JOHN COOPER

THE GREYHOUND

A NOVEL

DUNDURN
TORONTO

Project Editor: Michael Carroll
Editor: Nicole Chaplin
Design: Jesse Hooper
Printer: Webcom

Library and Archives Canada Cataloguing in Publication

Cooper, John, 1958-
    The greyhound / John Cooper.

Issued also in electronic format.
ISBN 978-1-55488-860-3

    I. Title.

PS8605.O665G74 2011   jC813'.6   C2010-906006-7

1   2   3   4   5   15   14   13   12   11

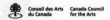 

We acknowledge the support of the **Canada Council for the Arts** and the **Ontario Arts Council** for our publishing program. We also acknowledge the financial support of the **Government of Canada** through the **Canada Book Fund** and **Livres Canada Books**, and the **Government of Ontario** through the **Ontario Book Publishing Tax Credit** and the **Ontario Media Development Corporation**.

Printed and bound in Canada.
www.dundurn.com

Dundurn Press
3 Church Street, Suite 500
Toronto, Ontario, Canada
M5E 1M2

Gazelle Book Services Limited
White Cross Mills
High Town, Lancaster, England
LA1 4XS

Dundurn Press
2250 Military Road
Tonawanda, NY
U.S.A. 14150

This book is dedicated to my grandson
Cooper Thomas Bevan
Run hard, run fast

ACKNOWLEDGEMENTS

THE AUTHOR WOULD like to acknowledge the following people and offer my sincere thanks for their continuing support: my agent Bill Hanna; Nicole Chaplin, my editor at Dundurn Press; Jerry Amernic; my wife, Maria, and my children, Melissa, Tyler, and Cole; Caleb Bevan; Yvonne Cooper; Denise Doogan (who was inspirational during a discussion of "tin can vans" a few years ago); and Larry Hill.

APRIL

DANNY WAS GLAD to be inside the church: outside, it was sunny and very warm. The church was cooler, if somewhat dank. He looked down from the second step of the stairs leading from the doorway to the basement, and watched his father work. Jack hadn't seen him yet.

Danny glanced outside where he'd parked his bike. He didn't have a lock for it, so he'd leaned it precariously against an iron railing, and it looked like it might fall over at any moment. He doubted it'd be a target for thieves: it was old, the paint on it had started to chip away, and one tire was going bald. *Who would want a bike like that anyway?* he thought. His father had told him to ride over to the church, and he'd toss the bike into the back of the van so they could drive home together, "the way we used to." But Danny could hardly remember a time when his father had driven him home from anything.

Danny watched as Jack took a big broom — the kind they used in schools, with a wide, flat brush and the handle dead centre — and pushed bright yellow sawdust down one side of the hallway, then up the other side.

Jack was working in the near dark; but the muted light that came through the basement windows made it seem cooler, and easier to work too. Down here in the dark, Danny imagined the colours pouring in through the stained-glass windows in the main part of the church upstairs, a mosaic of crayon colours splashed across the sanctuary toward the giant cross that hung at the end. He imagined the bright colours just touching Jesus's sculpted toes on the crucifix.

The wall going toward the community room was lined with posters. Bright colours and happy faces. African faces set against a backdrop of sparse trees and small cooking fires on redbrick earth. Far away. "Help us help our brothers and sisters in Darfur. Come out for our pancake breakfast."

Danny had been learning a lot about the issues that were creating so much pain and bloodshed for the people in the Darfur region of western Sudan. The war and suffering had seemed so far away, but they'd come right into Danny's life: the one friend he'd made since they'd moved was Ben, a refugee from Darfur who went to his school. Impossibly tall, Ben towered over everyone else, but was shy, kind of awkward, and exceedingly polite. He was still learning English, and was just as uncertain about his future in Canada as Danny was about his own new home. Danny was fifteen years old, and this town was new to him. Everything had changed and the past few months felt like falling down a hill and landing on concrete.

Danny could hear Father Rivera above, talking to someone in the church, somewhere in one of the pews. Telling them things would be all right.

His father looked focused, thick eyebrows pinched over his glasses. Danny knew this job wasn't what his old man wanted. His father's job at the church was, well, a job. He also worked at Danny's new high school and would shuttle between one job and the other, earning what he could for the family.

Danny struggled to understand what had happened to his father. But thinking about it was like swimming in the ocean and feeling the tide pull at you: no matter how hard you try to swim anywhere, you just get pulled farther and farther away, and eventually, you're just too tired to swim. You have to work with the current to get anywhere. Danny's thoughts about his father were like that. They pulled at him until they tired him out.

From what Danny knew of it, Jack's list of accomplishments was long: a former swimming champion, an advertising executive whose creativity helped sell the Whiz Bang laundry detergent that everyone was using ("*Whiz Bang! Your laundry never looked so good!*"), an amateur table-tennis champ, a former corporate supporter of the David Suzuki Foundation, and, when he was younger, a volunteer with Katimavik and Greenpeace. But now, pushing the broom, his face creased and mouth pinched, his knuckles shiny, bulbous, and bumpy from arthritis, Jack resembled an old bird, a hawk or an eagle maybe, that had been knocked out of the sky. Lost, alone, and hurt.

They'd moved to the new town after Jack had lost his job because of alcohol. His career was ruined. The family tried to hang onto their house in the old town. It was a big house, and the backyard that led down to a ravine that Danny used to imagine was a jungle. There was a ravine near the new home, *but it just isn't the same*, Danny thought.

But the family had to sell it. Rosemary, Danny's mother, was as a social worker and she just didn't bring in enough money. And, what's worse, Jack had driven drunk and hit someone, who had then sued him. So his finances were ruined even more. *They sued him good, or bad — good for them and bad for us*, Danny wrote in his journal. He was keeping the journal at the suggestion of the psychiatrist his parents were making him see. He wrote in it, but he didn't feel a sense of ownership of the words. *I'm just marking time. Pleasing other people instead of pleasing myself. All these notes are placeholders of someone else's life.*

Dad had grown up in this new town, and knew some people there, so they'd moved into a bungalow. The bungalow they moved into was small, and Danny had to share a washroom with his sister, Susan.

"It's nice. The house is nice," Rosemary had said. *Nice* was her word for anything, whether it was really *amazing-fantastic-incredible* or something that was *just so-so*. Danny had heard her say it so many times he felt it was tattooed into his brain: *NICE*. Like how his father had Chinese characters tattooed on his arm, which, he said, spelled out "looking for trouble." Where he got the tattoo, or why, Danny wasn't sure. But he imagined it wasn't so *nice*.

Yet nice was a word that Danny's mother loved. *Nice*. It was her way of smoothing things over. Be nice. Play nice. Isn't that *nice?* Danny rolled it around in his head. I'm nice. Susan's nice. According to Mom, the whole freakin' world is nice.

But Susan really wasn't nice. She was seventeen and ready to move out, and Danny didn't see much of her. She was going to university on a volleyball scholarship in the fall. She was taller than Danny, and had inherited her father's wiry frame: genetics were on her side. She always wore her black hair pulled back into a ponytail, and with her hardcore approach to everything, it wasn't a surprise that she was no pushover on the volleyball court. Her arms had grown from pipe-cleaner-thin and bony to lean, ropey, and muscular. She was ripped. Scary in a way. She looked the part of a student athlete, but her face had a hard edge to it, a threatening look that said "don't mess with me." Danny was on the receiving end of that look a lot. So Danny wouldn't mess with her. Susan was angry most of the time, which was good for volleyball. When she spiked the ball it would scare hell out of the opposing team. She was also really secretive, and Danny imagined her secrets locked away inside some vault inside her room, inside of her.

Danny's room overlooked the new house's backyard. There was a fence made of wooden planks, eight-feet high, one of those fences where, to see into the neighbour's backyard, you had to put your face right against the fence and look at an angle. There was a pine tree in one corner of the backyard, and Danny couldn't help but be impressed by it, even though it was just a pine tree: it had a thick trunk with rough, gnarled bark, and branches that were so large they looked like miniature Christmas trees. The whole thing was about fifty feet tall. He hated to think about chopping down something that was so strangely beautiful in its own way, but he couldn't escape the thought that you could probably get ten smaller trees out of the one big one.

Along the side of the yard was a weedy old vegetable garden. "Here's the job that you've been looking for," Dad had said shortly after they moved in. "You can clean up the veggie garden and grow some cucumbers and tomatoes for us this summer." Danny had just discovered an old piece of paper on which his great-grandfather had drawn, in pencil, the layout of a garden he'd planted back around the time of the First World War. In scratchy pencil but neat script it said, "Victory Garden." *That's what I need*, Danny thought, *a victory. And if it takes a garden to do it, so be it.*

"I'm good with that," Danny had replied. "We can put in some green peppers, too. Mom can use them." He was looking forward to becoming a backyard farmer that summer.

Danny was broken from his reverie when his father, seeing Danny standing on the stairs, smiled and called out, "Good to see you, Danny." His voice warm and thick. Danny felt his heart leap a little. No matter where he was, no matter how bad things might seem, Jack always seemed to be a hardcore optimist. "Let me finish up."

Ten minutes later he came up the stairs, paused to say goodbye to Father Rivera, and they were out the door. The sky had clouded over a bit and the air was cooler. They put the bike into the back of the van and drove home.

MAY

"I'M HOME!"

JACK'S VOICE BOOMED through the house. The budgie, Yellow Bird, chattered in the kitchen. Rosemary was outside hanging laundry and Danny was in his parent's washroom. He opened the medicine chest and looked at the small line-up of little bottles of prescription medicines that his father took — that he knew his father *had to take* now — though Danny was never told much about whatever it was that made his father grow a little more tired each day. *Must be old age*, he thought to himself.

He'd spent a chunk of his afternoon with his bedroom door closed, working on his computer, surfing the Internet for information on a school project. He wanted to go back to his room, but his father's voice was insistent — "Hey, where is everyone?" — and he changed his mind. Jack's voice sounded cheerier, healthier, which give Danny an odd little lift; he sensed that somehow, something was different. For months Jack had been quiet, more serious than ever before. He seemed to be focusing on some distant task or point in time, as if he were working off a debt.

Danny quickly went to his room and glanced at the computer screen. He saved the information he was looking for — on *The Old Man and the Sea* — and then switched it off. Dad was still talking in the hallway; his voice had gotten softer and more mellow, almost soothing. It wasn't the way he usually spoke to Rosemary, and anyway, his mom was still outside, but Jack was talking to someone, and Susan was still out.

Then he heard a small, thin whine, like a garden gate opening. It was a dog; a dog that was anxious or uncertain. Then he heard his father's low, even voice. "That's okay, girl, that's okay." He sounded honey-sweet and warm.

Danny ran out of his room. There, by the front door, was a tall, brindle greyhound, Jack firmly holding its leash. It turned its long nose to Danny and wagged its tail slightly. Dark, moist eyes looked at him, but also into him, like this skinny dog knew all of Danny's secrets.

"Isn't she a beauty?" Jack asked of no one in particular. The screen door from the backyard swung shut with a slam and Rosemary came in carrying an empty laundry basket. The clothespin she held between her lips fell with a clatter into the basket.

"Jack, what did I tell you about getting a dog?" she said. They'd obviously talked about it before, but Danny hadn't been privy to it.

"I said I was going to get a dog, I just didn't say what kind of dog," Jack answered. He reached down and scruffled the dogs ears. "Sit, girl." The dog sat. Her head reached almost to Jack's hip and she pushed her long nose against his hand. "See? She's already at home. What do you think of her? *I think* she's a beauty!"

Danny held back. He thought she was an ugly dog, scrawny and bony, and her skinny face reminded him of a rat. Her long skinny paws were like a rabbit's feet. He didn't understand why Dad would like this dog so much.

Mom was first with the questions.

"Where did you get her?"

"Tom Hill over in Mission House works with these dogs." Tom was an accountant, Dad had known him for a few years. "He has two himself. They're retired race dogs. They run for a couple of years, then they go to adoption agencies and they're placed in good homes."

Good homes, Danny thought. *Our home's a good home?* He looked around at the green wallpaper, the brown couch, and the way-too-small television (everyone else he knew had big, flat-screen TVs). He couldn't help but feel a little lift, though. The dog was looking right at him, straining her bony muzzle in his direction.

"See, she wants a friend. She's looking at you, pal."

"Does the dog have a name?" Rosemary asked.

"I'll leave that to Danny. When she was racing, her name was Long Shot. What do you think, Danno?"

"How about just 'Long?'" Danny said. "Like, so long, dog, gotta go, you loser."

"Come on, son, give her a chance. Every dog has a tail to wag and a tale to tell." He paused. Danny knew a story was coming. His father paused that way every time there was a story to tell.

"This dog reminds me of my time in Florida." They moved to the kitchen, and the dog moved quietly just behind Jack, as if she were looking forward to another of his long-winded stories. Long Shot sat at Jack's feet, then, got up and quietly moved over and put her head on Danny's leg, resting her chin on his thigh. Her dark eyes looked up at him searchingly.

Danny opened his diary the usual way:

Dear Craphead:

I don't get it about Dad. He is too quiet and too calm. He should be feeling like crap, but he seems to have his head together about stuff. He seems serene and it's creeping me out. He goes to his AA meetings and comes home and reads his John Irving book and talks to me like nothing happened. But we lost our house because of him! Dr. Feinman says I have to get over it, to forgive my father and recognize that I have to take control of my own life. Stop blaming people. I'm trying to do that, but why am I so angry?

The dog Dad got was ugly! Scrawny, and ribs poking out, and she has kind of a skinny face like a rat. I call her Ratface, but not when Mom and Dad are around.

Danny was in a rush. It was almost 7:00 a.m. and he had promised himself that he would be out running before seven. It was a cool morning, and the air smelled of dampness that could settle easily into one's bones. He finished eating his energy bar, gulped down some Gatorade, and bent down to lace up his shoes. He was so focused on getting ready to run that he didn't notice his mom standing in the kitchen doorway.

"Have you ever thought that you might be pushing yourself a little hard?" she asked. "We've only just moved here. You might want to relax a little more."

The remark irritated Danny, and his face showed it. "Mom, you don't have to be a social worker with me. You know I have to get back into a routine. There's a whole list of judo tournaments coming up and then a big tournament in a few months. I need to be ready." He pulled a piece of paper and a stubby pencil out of the pocket of his hoodie. He added a note to his list. "I have running to do, then weights, then breakfast, then school," he said as much to himself as to his mother.

"Just don't push yourself too hard." Rosemary's soft voice had already trailed off, lost in the wind, in the early morning twittering of birds and a lone dog barking on another street. Danny was already running up the street. He pushed the ear buds in as he jogged along the road, his thumb spinning the dial to find his favourite song. He veered slightly on the road, his shoes grinding on the finely crushed gravel as he moved to avoid tripping over a fat cat that lived two houses down. The cat was crouched by the curb, its ears laid back, watching a robin on a front lawn. The robin danced around the lawn, bobbing its head, listening for worms, and the cat was engrossed, watching it. Danny narrowly missed the cat's tail, earning a warning hiss. *What's with these cats around here?* he thought. *They act like they own the whole neighbourhood.*

Danny passed an old rail fence along one property. Grey squirrels chased each other along the top, doing acrobatic leaps into the bushes that ran parallel to the fence. One of the squirrels, its tail twitching like a battery-operated toy, chattered nervously as Danny ran by, perhaps warning him away from the nest it was building in the nearby maple tree. The houses in this neighbourhood were old, but not so old that they were falling apart. They stretched along the road like senior citizens enjoying a rare bit of November sunshine before bracing themselves for the icy blast of winter.

As he listened to his music, Danny thought about the goals he had set for himself: become a better judoka; learn to garden like his great-grandfather; get control of his temper, which seemed to be explosive at times; and forgive his father. He settled into a strong, rhythmic pace. Some of his goals would be harder to accomplish, but nothing seemed to be easy. They were all vague, cagey ghosts that taunted him.

Danny's new school was clean and antiseptic, its walls and floors were whitewashed and smelled of toilet-bowl cleaner and Windex. The lockers stretched forever, in long sections painted in primary colours. Every few lockers, one was decorated for someone's birthday. And the student-of-the-month would have their locker painted in swirls of blue, red, orange, green, yellow.

Here I am, in my old man's old high school, Danny thought. The walls of the hallway that stretched from the cafetorium (it was both a cafeteria and an auditorium) to the gymnasium, were hung with photographs of the school's best and brightest, the jocks and scholars who had won awards or who were otherwise recognized for their achievements. There were signs announcing the school's upcoming Frantically Funny concert and show, a combination of dancing, sketch comedy, and especially music, under the direction of the black-bearded and scowlingly bombastic Mr. Harkness. He was an old hippie who, for thirty years, had guided the talented and less-than-talented music students through the intricacies of coaxing music from oboes, clarinets, saxophones, and other instruments, and who never once winced at the scratching or squealing of an ill-played note. This was one of those stereotypical schools, where the teaching faculty was comprised of old hippies and draft dodgers — all corduroy pants, lumberjack shirts, corduroy pants, rimless glasses, and grey beards. There was also a sprinkling of young teachers, fresh out of teachers' college.

Danny wandered down the hallway, trying to avoid bumping into other students while looking for his father's photograph along the way. He couldn't find it. Jack had won a handful of gold medals in swimming. He rarely spoke about it — only when he was trying to gently persuade Danny to set some realistic goals for himself — but Danny knew he was proud of his achievements. (What Danny didn't know was that his father's photograph was lost in a fire in a supply room many years before.)

Schools all have the same theme, he wrote in his journal. *The geeks and jocks and brains, lined up smiling for generation after generation to see.* The school was set up as a series of blocks, different buildings connected by glass-enclosed breezeways. It was designed so that every room received natural sunlight. *Like big clear giant Lego blocks. You can't hide, you can't run. You are caught in a transparent cube, with the other rats.* The students moved from class to class in groups of two or three, some alone, like Danny, shifty-eyed and moving quickly through the crowds, trying to be transparent.

Danny was relieved to see Ben (though he didn't act it) after second period one day; to see Ben's familiar face in a wave of students, moving easily through the crowd. They fell into a pattern of meeting each other in the hall-way and heading to third period together. The teachers were a mixed lot, most old and dusty, like books left on the shelf too long, but occasionally an oldster would be bright. Mr. Jackson, the history teacher, for instance. *It's like he's still a young person. Like his brain hasn't aged*, Danny thought. *Jackson is cool. He just seems to get what students are thinking about, what they need to know. History is being created today*, he told us. *You are creating your own personal history. That history is part of who we are as a society. You would do well to think about carving out a place for yourself, making the most of what you have, and making a contribution to our shared history.*

THE DOJO

Danny was uncertain about going to a new judo club, but there was no sense asking his parents to drive him to his old club — it was just too far away. And his parents certainly weren't putting any pressure on him to continue practising; in fact, he'd even been wavering for a while about continuing. But when he met the head of the club, a man who called himself only "Sensei Bob," any fears he may have had began to evaporate.

"See? How could you not like this guy?" Jack would say later. He had met Bob at the community centre and they'd talked about Danny joining the club.

Sensei Bob was a man of average height and build. There was nothing in the way he carried himself of the sense of raw brute power that Danny had seen in other judo practitioners. In other places, Danny had seen *judo-kus* who always behaved with a sense of power, arrogance, and superiority, hefting it the way a father carries a growing child: with a self-indulgent knowledge of his own strength. Bob was not like that.

Sensei Bob was quiet, but confident, with strong hands, and a firm grip as he grabbed hold of a student's *gi* in a training, talking through all of the movements of tossing an opponent to get his point across. Round spectacles perched on an imperfect nose, he had a scrubby soul patch below his lower lip, and his shock of dark hair was in disarray, making him look like an aging student, someone who was always learning.

Danny's father spoke highly of Bob. "Bob is the kind of teacher all good teachers want to be," he'd said. "He gets people to do things that they wouldn't normally want to do, working them hard in a way that makes them glad to have done that hard work." Bob had drew pupils from all over town, and some came from even farther away to learn from him. Several students would drive two hours just for an hour and a half of practise with Bob.

"The dojo is fairly quiet this time of day," Sensei Bob told Danny. "Most of our students come in the evening. But it's good to have students here right after school. We like to make full use of the facility." He smiled crookedly. "After the judo students are gone some old ladies come in to do yoga." He laughed. "They love to come and do some stretching. Happy old folk. In the summer we have a big festival, and all of the people who come here, young and old, get together. Eat tea fondants and drink lemonade and iced tea. It's a very nice time.

"That's Stan, one of my more senior students," Bob said, gesturing to a hulking teenager with a brown belt, who looked around eighteen or nineteen, working with a group of younger students. They were working through a series of basic judo moves. The walls behind the group were panelled with wood, arranged in a brickwork pattern of cubes and rectangles in what must have been considered artistically pleasing back when the building was constructed. Danny had been told the building had been here when his father was a kid, and he doubted it had changed much in the intervening half-century or so. It was like the architecture in the old library in Danny's hometown, and recalling this detail made him a little sad. The other walls were built of solid blocks of concrete and painted with several coats of white and orange —the kind of paint that dried to a shiny, polished sheen, like the glazed icing on a cookie. There was Japanese lettering painted in black on one of the walls. "It says 'Here we work' in Japanese," Sensei Bob explained. On a far wall, and positioned high up, about eight feet above the mat, was a black and white photograph of Jigoro Kano, the creator of judo. The final wall was glass, with several sliding doors. Light from outside filtered through the pine trees that lined an outdoor patio that was outfitted with a few round plastic tables and a picnic table that looked like it had been there for a hundred years. The natural light gave the dojo a feeling of being bigger than it was.

The *tatami*, the thick woven mats on which the students practised, were bright, colourful — several of them were arranged in a square in the centre of the dojo. Around these were evergreen-coloured mats, arranged like the tiles of a mosaic. Even before he entered the dojo, Danny could hear a distinctive *Shhhh-thump, shhhh-thump* of students tossing each other onto the mats, their bare feet sliding across the textured surface of the *tatami* before they threw — or were thrown by — their sparring partner.

"You have a good build for a *judo*," Sensei Bob said, glancing at Danny's shoulders. "Low centre of gravity." He reached out to take hold of the heavy quilted sleeve of Danny's *gi*. "Here, grab my *gi*." Danny did as he was told. "Steady yourself. Yes, good grip. Try throwing me. Try the *osoto-gari*. Something basic." Danny quickly moved one foot inside, into the space between Bob's feet, sweeping it down by Bob's ankle, turning and moving, tugging downwards on the sleeve of Bob's gi. He could feel the fluidity of the motion, like water coursing over a dam. He moved into the space formerly occupied by Bob, shifting and easily tossing his new teacher onto the mat. *Shhh-thump*. Bob sprung up.

"Good, good. Your technique is not bad at all. A bit of work to do, yes, but you will do fine."

DANNY PLANTS HIS GARDEN

The next day, Danny set to work planting the tomatoes, onions, green peppers, and cucumbers that would be the mainstay of his garden. He and Jack bought old railway ties to use as a frame for the garden, and Danny spent the day before turning and working the soil. He sweated for hours to get the soil to loosen up: it had a lot of clay in it, making it tough to turn. He added bags of manure to it, and Father Rivera brought over bushel baskets of topsoil. Behind the wheel of his navy blue pickup truck, the padre didn't look like a parish priest. He was wearing blue jeans and a black T-shirt and looked the part of a landscaper. He had on an old straw hat that reminded Danny of the straw hat that his grandfather used to wear fishing. Grandpa had been dead for ten years and Danny barely remembered his face, but he never forgot the old hat.

"Hi-ho, Danny," Father Rivera called. Danny and Jack came over to take the baskets of topsoil to the backyard and dump them on the garden.

"Keep working, my son," Father Rivera smiled. "You're making some good progress. This earth around these parts is tough, at first, but when you find the right combination, it will give you the best tomatoes, red as rubies, fat, and full of flavour, and crispy cucumbers. And you remember to invite me over for a salad when they're ripe!" The Father tipped his hat and left Danny to continue his work. He added some peat moss to the mix of topsoil and manure: he'd heard that peat moss would help break up the clay.

He was kneeling down and getting ready to plant, when his mother joined him. "Here's a good way of figuring out where you want to put the plants," she said. "Cucumbers grow like crazy, so you'll want to tie them to wooden stakes. That'll train them up so they won't sprawl all over and cover the other plants. The tomatoes can have a corner, opposite to the cucumbers so they won't be overshadowed. The peppers can be in front, so they get some good sun." She looked at the sky, reassessing the position of the garden. "This spot will get some good afternoon sun. Hmm ... the onions need some space in front of the peppers." She put the plants in their little pots in place.

They began digging the holes and planting the seedlings. Danny liked doing things with his mother. She never judged him, never corrected him unless he asked for her input. She was a quiet, diligent worker, and Danny imagined how great she must be at work, dealing with people high on drugs or angry or depressed, and how incredibly strong she must be, not to get angry or upset. Suddenly, he found himself asking a question he didn't plan to ask. He just blurted it out. "Why did Dad start drinking?"

Rosemary didn't turn to him but stayed focused on getting the plants into the ground. He could see the edge of her face, etched against the brown soil, and the expression on it changed, as if a shadow had passed over it suddenly. She looked like the daisies that grew wildly in the spring, bursts of yellow, white, and green, but then began to fade by mid-summer, seemingly before their time. She seemed this way more often since his dad's drinking began to haunt the family. It was like a ghost that just wouldn't go away, that kept knocking at the door, causing the floor to creak, waking them up at night with its lonely moans.

"Your father started drinking when he was young. Some people get into bad habits, and then those habits get out of control. And then they create excuses, or reasons, for pursuing those habits. It's just like that. I wish sometimes I could tell you that something awful happened in your dad's life that made him want to escape or kill his pain, but as far as I know that wasn't the case. Your dad started on a path of behaviour, and neither he, nor anybody else, stopped him. I met him at a time when he wasn't drinking that much, and he had certain qualities that I liked so I chose to ignore some of his less stellar qualities."

"Like the drinking...." Danny was quiet for a minute.

"The first time I saw your father, he was swimming. He won the bronze medal at the regional finals in the butterfly. You should have seen him churning through the water. He had a great swimmer's build — the wide shoulders and contoured body, like all of his muscles were specially designed for his sport. He was young and strong and had these bright hazel eyes that I thought were just, well, cute." Danny shuddered. It was weird hearing his mother call his father "cute." "I was a lifeguard at the community rec centre for the summer. Athletes trained there in the off hours in the Olympic-sized pool, after the regular crowd went home. He was a lot older than me, but he was intriguing and funny and smiled a lot. I went out with him a couple of times and he was a very sweet, very caring young man. Being with him was like … it was like the first time you see fireflies on a spring night, you know? When it's warm and gentle and the air is sweet and the sun is just starting to go down, and as dusk settles in, there's suddenly a hundred sparkling, blinking green and yellow lights in the bulrushes by the pond, and in the background there's a chorus of frogs trilling and croaking. And even though you feel like you've seen them a hundred times before, it's still an amazing feeling to see the fireflies again.… Anyway, your dad and I didn't see each other again for years after that. And by then he'd been overseas, worked for a not-for-profit organization that helped people in developing countries start businesses and become self-sufficient, and was coaching swimming. Your father was already well into middle age when you were born. His life had been, at times, very unpleasant. Maybe it's because I'm a social worker and I have to be an active listener, but your father opened up to me about a lot of things. Maybe it's just because I was the first person he could trust in his life. But he told me a lot, and some of it I would have a hard time sharing with you: a lot of it was hard and full of suffering, but your father always struggled to help other people."

Danny thought of the snippets of stories of his father's experiences as a worker in central Africa, helping build houses and wells and installing pumps and teaching children to read, and how he would stop short of describing anything that even approached violence. But there was violence, Danny knew. It was like the violence that marked Ben's life, which spread across his face like a shadow when he described the janjaweed.

Rosemary looked across the yard at the neighbour's cat peeking through the fence. "I hope that cat doesn't poop in my flowers," she said before continuing her story about Jack. "When he was young his own father was a drinker, and his mother was one of those women who create the image of a relationship where everything is okay, rather than truthful. Your grandfather would often be out drinking, so your dad would spend a lot of time on his own. One day when he was ten years old, his father challenged him to swim twenty laps in the pool at the community centre. Your father did it, and liked it, and found something he could put his energy into. He became a great swimmer, and eventually made it to the national level. He just narrowly missed the cut for the Olympics, he was *that good*.

"Your father was always striving to be the best, and he's easily disappointed, so instead of using failure to build himself up, he let it drag him down. Alcohol becomes a refuge, a hiding place, for a lot of people. They use it to hide from themselves. So, despite what he saw and what he knew, and how good he could be, your father began a pattern of behaviour that was *not good*, despite having grown up around someone whose own behaviour had hurt his family so much. He drank, and then stopped, and then started again, and then stopped. Anyway, he was better for several years, and then your grandfather died and your dad didn't take it well. Despite what happened when he was younger, your father was deeply attached to him. When he died, your dad set off on a path of self-destructive behaviour."

Danny's eyes felt moist. "I'm glad he stopped."

"So am I. Every day, he lives with the difficult task of recovery. Each and every day he struggles. He does appreciates our support, but he knows that this is something he has to do on his own. Life is precious, and he's working on it."

Danny remembered an incident that took place a few days earlier: a bee had gotten inside the house and Susan wanted to kill it with a flyswatter. But he'd taken an old Mason jar, waited until the bee landed, and captured it, letting it go outside. Later his father told him there was an old legend from a tribe in the Yukon, the Tagish, that said if you save an animal's life there's a chance it will return the favour someday.

"Kind of like *Androcles and the Lion*, the guy who took the thorn out of the lion's paw, and then the lion rewarded him later?" Danny asked.

"Kind of like that," Jack had said. "So you never know. That bee might just help you out someday."

His mother's voice interrupted his thought: "Life is precious," she repeated, her voice distant, like she was lost in thought.

"That's true." Danny eased a tomato plant into a neat round hole he'd dug with his scoop. He carefully pushed soil in around the roots and patted the earth down around the base of the plant.

"Almost done," his mother said and smiled. "Remember to give them lots of water."

"I will."

A few years earlier, around the time that things were starting to look especially bad for Jack, a greyhound called Babs was giving birth to a litter of seven pups at a dog kennel in Florida.

"A lucky number, seven," said Pops Mahoney, the kennel owner. He was a wiry man of medium height, with a sunburned face and leathery arms tanned brown from thirty years in the Florida sun. He'd come from Killarney, Ireland, the son of a greyhound racer, who was also the son of a greyhound racer.

"Greyhound racing's in my blood," he'd said to a *Tampa Tribune* reporter many years before when the reporter was doing a feature story on Mahoney's kennel. "You can't get it out, once it's in. It's been programmed into my DNA. I *just know* the look of a good running dog."

It was true. For thirty years Mahoney, who ran a contracting business building many of the state's highways and bridges, also ran dogs at the Tampa Greyhound Track. He had bred and raced dozens of top dogs over the years, and he was proud of the fact that he was gentle with his dogs. "I believe in lettin' the good of the dog come out. Lettin' it do what it loves to do — run — without having to be urged or forced into doin' it." He was thinking about that line as he watched Babs give a little push, and a wet puppy emerged into the world. One of the pups was bigger than the rest, a tough female that, even deaf and blind (she wouldn't start to see or hear for ten days), was pushing the others away, struggling to be top dog.

"Aye, this one's a keeper," Mahoney said to Babs. Thunder rolled across the sky as he looked out at the palmetto trees on his property. He reached down and picked up the struggling wet bag of fur. "Aye, you'll be a strong one. I can *feel* it in you."

The young, brindle pup did not disappoint. Within two weeks she had her eyes open and was pushing her way around the whelping box. And a few weeks later she was tumbling with her littermates on the concrete floor of the kennel. Mahoney carefully chose the dogs that he wanted to run and registered them with the National Greyhound Association. The others were adopted out.

His favourite, the strong, brindle female, he named Mahoney's Long Shot. She was taller and stronger than the rest, and while he didn't expect her to be a big winner for Mahoney's Irish Kennels, he hoped she might do well. At three months, Mahoney neatly put a number inside each dog's left ear with a tattoo gun. In the right ear he tattooed the pup's birth information. "Ah, Long Shot, you will do me justice," he said, and smiled. The surf pounded miles away. The other dogs in the kennel made the *rooing* sound so particular to greyhounds. Long Shot licked Mahoney's nose.

Long Shot grew fast, leaping in great greyhound bounds ahead of her littermates and demonstrating the urge to run. She grew into a brown-and-grey hound with a smattering of chocolate-brown and coal-black spots sprinkled across her flanks. She was taller by a head than her siblings who had also been chosen to race, Mahoney's Little Bobby, a square, eager male pup, and Gracie's Lark, taller, almost the size of Long Shot, but shyer.

One afternoon, she was playing in an enclosure with her siblings, tackling Bobby, who would easily throw her off, and then Gracie, who was quick to *roo* and then scamper away — all of them chasing after a red rubber ball Rufus casually tossed in their direction. Rufus was Mahoney's sixteen-year-old son. He looked after the day-to-day needs of the dogs. It wasn't an easy job, either. Unlike his father, the red-haired lad Rufus was tall and built like a chunk of ocean coral, carved by the Gulf winds into a hefty and capable linebacker on the high school football team. After school, Rufus would head home to tend to the dogs, which could number up to thirty at any given time.

Long Shot, Bobby, and Gracie's Lark, named for Mahoney's wife, were the last of the litter. By eight months, all three had learned to come, sit, and stay — the basic commands a dog needed to get by with people. And they had been "gentled" a good deal — cuddled and played with by Rufus, his sister Melanie, and their friends.

It was important for greyhounds to get along with people, given that at the track any number of different people might handle them. They had to be able to be relaxed so they wouldn't snap.

At a year, Long Shot and her siblings were taken to the training track, a red, dirt, oblong roundabout that circled a patch of crabgrass, kudzu, and shrubbery, enclosed by a chain-link fence, at the back of Mahoney's property. A lure was dragged in front of the dogs to get them interested. It didn't take any urging to get Long Shot to chase the lure, she went after it without hesitation.

"Aye, she's a fine chaser," said Mahoney, taking off his cloth cap and running a hand over his head.

"I think she's going to be an early breaker," he added, alluding to the fact that some dogs would break out ahead of the pack early, setting a challenging pace. "Not much of a looker, mind you," he said, looking that the dog's long skinny nose — long even for a greyhound. "But she's got the legs, taller, longer even than old Gertie's Pride. Remember her?" He liked to reminisce about Gertie, one of his early dogs and a big winner.

"That was before my time, Pops."

Long Shot's early life was spent running, eating, sleeping, playing with other dogs, and sometimes fighting with them, but only to assert herself as the leader of the pack. She would often strain at her leash, eager to get into the box at the end of the track, ready to race. She was like a slick bolt of supercharged energy. Her muscles would ripple and tense, messages firing like spark plugs, *ping-ping-ping*, her paw pads tapping on the brown sand, leg muscles coiling, waiting to spring out of the gate, waiting for the mechanical rabbit to come whirring around the inside of the track. Then it would come in sight, until it was twenty feet down the track and *ka-chung!!* the gates would open and a flood of pure, raw dog energy would burst forth, pouring down the track after the rabbit.

Long Shot would pound ahead of the others, urging herself by brute force and finesse along the rail, as close as she could get to the rabbit. Sand would fly and her muscles would pump, pushing her forward harder it seemed than she ever ran before. The sound of the crowd at the track would be just rough background noise, a roller coaster of sound that would go higher and higher as the dogs came around the first turn, into the straightaway, around the second turn and into the home stretch. And then the race would be over, the dogs slowed down, dripping saliva from their tongues, panting and huff-huff-huffing as they were led away.

Mahoney pampered his dogs, because he was very attached to them. They always got water, a soft cushion, and a toy teddy bear, as well as delicious food, after a race. But with Long Shot winning and her value going up, there came a time when an offer was just too good to refuse. He reluctantly sold her to a man name Bibbs, who turned out to be a decent owner, and treated her with respect, though not with the same affection that Mahoney brought to each of his pups.

Mahoney once said to Rufus, "I was there for her birth. It is a different thing altogether, lad, when you've raised it from a whelp. I can't expect a man to love her the way I did."

THE PSYCHIATRIST'S OFFICE

There was a good reason that Danny was going to see a psychiatrist. He reminded himself of it every time he went through Dr. Feinman's door.

The first time he went to the psychiatrist's office, the inside of it didn't match his expectations at all. There was no rosewood panelling or heavy bookcases heaving with the texts by Sigmund Freud and Carl Jung, with a bronze statue of a long-dead psychiatrist as a paper weight, holding down a stack of research papers. Nor was there a dark wood desk covered in pictures of children with braces lining up at the tennis court, or the psychiatrist himself standing at the helm of a boat, with cottages along the shoreline in the background. There was one photograph, though, of a girl holding a bunch of daisies. She was about Danny's age, with auburn hair and dark eyes. *She's hot*, Danny thought to himself.

"That's my daughter. Her name's Emma," Dr. Feinman said with a smile.

Danny quickly put on a cool, disinterested pose. "Oh," was all he said.

The movie-inspired image of a psychiatrist's office that Danny had in his mind was no match for this shrink's office. ("Do you like it when people call you a 'shrink?'" Danny had asked at their first meeting. Feinman laughed. "Like it? I love it!" he said). It was all chrome and light colours, pastel shades.

There were modern prints on the walls, and the furniture was shiny, like a race car. A rubber tree sat in a corner of the room. And the psychiatrist was not what Danny had expected either; he expected short and surly, with a bushy grey beard, middle-aged and dour, wearing a tweed jacket and smelling like an old sock drawer. Instead he met a tall, athletic man in a plaid shirt, his head shaved so clean that it caught a glint of light from the environmentally friendly bulbs in the ceiling fixture. Dr. Feinman wore wire-rimmed, round-lens glasses that reminded Danny of the poster of John Lennon that Dad had in his study in their old house. He had a gold earring in his left ear, just like Danny's dad. It made him look a bit like a lost pirate, lost in an air-conditioned office with nice furniture, his pirate ship miles away on the open ocean.

Dr. Feinman was bright and cheery. "Let's talk about the last week, Danny." He didn't use a notepad — that was the other difference between him and the movie shrink Danny had expected — and he was sipping a cup of rose-hip tea. Danny could smell it, even from six feet away.

"There's not much to tell," he said. "My dad brought home a dog. A greyhound. It used to run at the track. He's crazy about her." He had started to anticipate Dr. Feinman's questions. The next one would be "And what do you think about her?"

"I don't know if I like her or not." Danny answered before Dr. Feinman could even ask.

"What's happening at school?"

"Things are okay. Math is getting better, actually." For a long time, he had been angry about math — he used to be so good at it, but over the last few months things had been slipping. He was being tutored by a wise-cracking senior student who was racking up community service hours, and who was actually getting him to like math again.

They talked about what Danny called "nothing" for a while — Feinman asking mundane questions, Danny given dull, rote answers.

Then, Fienman asked, "Do you still think about what happened with your dad?"

He was referring to the suicide attempt his dad had made a year before. A business deal had gone bad, and Dad had tried to kill himself in the garage of the old house by running a hose from the exhaust pipe into the car. Or that was the story Danny told himself when he wanted to pretend that his dad was troubled, maybe even trying to be noble, in a morbid way. The truth was that he'd driven into the garage, drunk, after spending the evening with some advertising people. He'd closed the garage door, and fallen asleep with the motor running. Their old dog Benny had barked and woken everyone up — everyone except Dad — when the carbon monoxide had started to seep into the house. Nauseated and woozy, Danny and Susan stumbled into the front yard. Mom opened the garage door and pulled Dad out. Danny couldn't believe her strength, lugging a big man like Dad, pulling him out onto the front lawn.

Dad coughed. "Whaaa! What!" he said as he woke to the cold, clean autumnal air at three o'clock in the morning.

The event had haunted Danny's nightmares, chasing him down, a cold, lean savage beast that wouldn't let him go. Reliving the possibility that they all might have died in their sleep, instead of being woken by a barking, scrappy little part-terrier-part-bloodhound with his *whoop-whoop-arooo* howling bark.

That was part of why he'd come to Dr. Feinman.

JUNE

AS A RULE, retired greyhounds weren't big runners. They preferred walking quietly, perhaps because they had spent so much time running in their first three or four years of life. Long Shot really liked walks, and Danny was only too happy to oblige. And sometimes Ben accompanied them. Their walks were usually uneventful, but one day something happened when Danny and Ben took Long Shot to the high school grounds for her walk.

Behind the high school there was an old quarter-mile track of soft red cinders. It was overgrown with weeds and dandelions that spread wildly, as if a giant had cast a few handfuls of yellow gumdrops across the green field. Beetles and other small insects winged about; big, shiny, blue dragonflies patrolled the area in the warm late spring sun. Jackrabbits scurried through the grass, and the occasional red fox scampered across the grass, darting through the tall weeds after field mice.

Danny was holding Long Shot's leash loosely in one hand. He was looking off at the yellow brick high school, on the other side of the long driveway that wound around the school to the back parking lot, wondering what school would be like in the fall. Suddenly he realized he was no longer holding the leash.

Ben yelled, "Hey, man, you let the dog go. Look! There she goes!" They'd been walking along the edge of the track, and now Long Shot was loping down to the track, a rabbit in her sight. Danny knew this was a bad thing: greyhounds are not supposed to go off leash. They're easily distracted by moving object, and often take off, deaf to their owner's pleas to come back.

"Crap! We gotta get her! What are my folks gonna say?"

Danny and Ben started running after her, but there was no way they could catch her — or keep her in sight for very long. Within seconds the dog was halfway down the track, and Danny figured she would just keep on running, past the line of maple trees that stretched along the edge of the school grounds, across Mason Street, and far, far away. He'd be looking for her for hours.

But then a strange thing happened. Instead of taking off, away from the track, Long Shot seemed to melted into the moist air, her body a blur of honey gold, a smudge of pastel colour against the red cinders and emerald grasses as she made a perfect turn along the curve of the track.

"Look at that," said Ben, scratching his head. "She thinks she's racing again! She's going all the way around the track!"

They both stopped, watching in amazement as Long Shot, framed by the tall grasses in the centre portion of the track before disappearing behind a stand of tall weeds, ran elegantly, gracefully, and quickly around the track. She completed one lap, and then tired, and with a satisfied look on her face, she trotted up to Danny and sat down, chest heaving. She nudged his hand with her nose, looking for approval and a pat on the head.

He was supposed to be upset, with himself and with the dog for running away, but he was more relieved than anything else.

Besides, how could Danny be mad? "That was quite a run, girl," he said, massaging her ears. "You still have a lot of energy left in you, don't you?"

Every day after that, they would go back to the abandoned track behind the high school. Long Shot would run around the track, and Ben would take off after her, following far behind: no one could keep up with her.

"Why all the running?" Danny asked.

"I'm going to try out for track and field next year. I need to work at it."

Ben didn't have to work at it too hard, from what Danny could tell. He had a long stride, and his lean frame moved easily along the track, his arms swinging slightly, like he was being carried by the soft spring breeze. He ran as if in slow motion, so effortlessly, but when coming around the far turn, Danny could see that Ben was moving much faster than he'd originally thought. He ran around the track four times, then jogged steadily around half of the track to cool down. By this time Long Shot had finished her run and was lying in the grass, snuffling after a bug.

"Where did you learn to run like that?" Danny asked, as Ben took a long drink from a bottle of Gatorade.

"In Darfur, we used to run everywhere. From one end of the village to the other. From village to village. We were little kids who loved to run. Then…" and his voice dropped.

"Then what?"

"Then…" Ben's voice trailed off again, his eyes taking on a haunted look. It was clearly not a subject he was comfortable with. "Then the janjaweed came."

Danny was about to say, "What's that?" but Ben had obviously sensed the question coming.

"The janjaweed are the riders on horseback with guns and gasoline. They came to our village. I ran into the bushes. I ran for what seemed like all night."

As Ben told his story, Danny wondered at how he'd survived. The raiding party killed his father and mother, his sisters and brothers, and those who weren't killed, disappeared. He ran into the scrubby bushes that surrounded the village, running from the burning huts and screaming people and the crackling sound of gunfire. He ran into the night. Exhausted, he fell asleep on the brown earth several miles from the village. The next morning he awoke to find a member of the janjaweed standing over him, speaking in Arabic, a language he did not understand. He was taken to a compound, forced to work for his food, separated from his family. He was only ten years old. A year later he escaped, following a trail to an open road, where he was picked up by United Nations aid workers, then taken to a refugee camp. Two years later, he was lucky enough to be relocated to Canada. He found a home with the Logan family, learned English, and began attending school.

"That's a wild story," said Danny. "It must have been very tough. Saying goodbye to your country, to your village …"

"Very tough. But one of my teachers, Mr. Ogbuwe, says we have to realize that our strength is something that is always in us. It never really leaves. We have to listen for it, to know when to find it, when we are faced with danger or trouble."

Danny's attention was diverted by the dog. Long Shot yawned, wagged her tail slightly, then lifted herself up off the ground, stretching.

"Time to go home," said Danny.

"It's good to *have a home*," said Ben, and his voice was full of emotion. "Good to have family. It's good to *be home.*"

THE TEXAN

A big Texan named Dave Langley was mulling over the email he'd just read at his training facility outside of Arlen. The evening sky over Texas was stained a multi-coloured hue, from ocean blue to a rich purple and streaks of orange cloud stretched away to the horizon and the scrub brush around his compound. The small dog track was splashed with spots of dying yellow sunshine.

"Ah, evening," Dave said to himself. He was sitting on the porch of his home, which his grandfather had built. "Built to last," Grandpa Langley had said, and it did. Constructed as it was of quarried stone and large logs from a forest far beyond the city limits, and put together by the senior Langley, who had made his money in cattle ranching and oil, and his team of superb carpenters and craftsmen, the house had stood for almost a hundred years. Inside, massive timbers formed struts across the ceiling, and a stone fireplace was the centrepiece of the place. It was big: as big as Dave, as big as the family he grew up in, big enough for his own brood. Three generations of Langleys had lived there, raising cattle, growing grain, investing in oil, and eventually, racehorses and greyhounds.

Dave sipped on sweetened ice tea and stretched, putting his long legs up on the porch railing. A sleek fawn greyhound with little spots of black and brown wandered over to Dave and nudged Dave's hand for a scratch around the ears. "That's a good boy, Dynamo," Dave said, gently kneading the dog's ears. The dog yawned and looked at Dave through its dark chocolate eyes, all sweetness.

The email, from a close associate who lived a thousand miles away, was intriguing. "Dave: remember that race you wanted to run? You were looking for the best of the last few years? Mahoney's dog Long Shot, the big female that was handed off and then adopted, was seen just a couple of days ago by a buddy of mine. Racing around a high school track, no less!"

Dave had called and gotten details. Then he called Mahoney. "That old pup of yours, the one that won all that money, she's still rarin' to go."

Mahoney was less excited. "She can't run anymore, the old gal's not got the stamina to take to the track again."

But Langley wouldn't be put off. "I told you I was going to bring the best together again. This is the race of the decade."

"Don't you mean the race of the century?"

"Naw. Things happen too fast now. You never know what's going to happen next. I'll just call it the race of the decade."

While they discussed the details of getting the best of the best together, Mahoney remained skeptical, but Dave was adamant: "It'll be a great show for the racing industry and especially for the fans."

"For a cattle man you've got quite the flair for dramatization," Mahoney said with a laugh.

"Heck, my family hasn't been in cattle for a long time," said Dave. "But the flair you'll see will be in us having just a regular rootin' tootin' wonderful race," he added, letting his Texas drawl come out. "I think Long Shot and these other dogs we'll track down still have a flair for running."

IN THE BASEMENT

Jack had arranged some office furniture to create a study in the basement, a little alcove set in from the bottom of the stairs. A corkboard was covered with yellow and pink notes, pinned to the earth-coloured cork-like square butterflies. Cryptic writing in his father's messy script revealed nothing to Danny, except that one was obviously a to-do list:

- Clean eaves
- Danny to judo
- Susan to volleyball and track
- Walk Long
- Plan next steps

He was always planning for a return to advertising, but Danny wondered whether it was ever going to happen. He looked at a plaque on the wall; gold lettering on a blue background, posted to a wood backing, and laminated:

> God grant me the serenity
> To accept the things I cannot change
> The Courage to change the things I can
> And the Wisdom to know the difference.

It was the Alcoholics Anonymous credo.

Danny once went with his mother to pick his father up after a meeting at a room in the local community centre. The exposed brick was whitewashed, the chairs were straight-backed and steel and very uncomfortable-looking, they made Danny wonder if the members of AA were made to suffer for the sins by sitting ramrod-straight for several hours, a few times a week. Cigarette smoke hung in the air like a sick, blue fog and burned his eyes. He could smell burnt coffee coming from an enormous stainless-steel coffee urn on a plastic tablecloth-covered side table. The recovering alcoholics all seemed pretty cheery, but some of them just seemed grateful for the companionship of others who were shaking what Dad called, "the monkey off their backs."

"Alcohol is like this little monkey that sits on your shoulder and whispers in your ear. You keep feeding it, hoping it will go away. But it chatters and screams in your ear and bites at your neck and pokes its dirty little fingers in your eyes. You keep feeding it, but instead of leaving the monkey only gets bigger and bigger and you get weaker. You can't hear the people around you, the people who care, for all the chattering and screaming the monkey does. It becomes your life, and even though you hate it, you keep feeding it, even when it craps all over you. Eventually it kills you. The monkey." Danny didn't like the graphic way his father talked about his alcoholism: it always gave him the chills.

"So what about the monkey now?" Danny asked on the ride home.

"If it doesn't kill you, you stop feeding it. It sits there on your shoulder and you starve it. Stop giving it what it wants. It gets quiet, stops its chattering. But you have to tell yourself that it never really goes away. It's going to be perched on my shoulder as long as I live, which is just as well, because it's a reminder of what I need to do for myself and my family. And that's to *not drink*."

Danny felt a chill again, remembering the incident.

Also on the corkboard was a postcard of the Tampa Greyhound Track. "Greetings from Tampa, Florida, home of the country's top greyhounds." The photograph was of a mass of dogs, bursting around the curve of the track, a wave of green, red, and yellow jackets. Danny could see the power in their stride, and thought of Long Shot's grace and speed.

"Tampa was quite a time in my life," Jack said, startling Danny who hadn't heard his footsteps on the stairs. He looked at his father's face. Jack coughed, his skin looked ashy, and the lines on his face were etched more deeply into his skin than Danny remembered. He tapped the postcard on the corkboard. "The track was full of characters. There was this one guy, Renaldo, who was from the Bahamas. He hung around the track, from open until close. Wore a flowered shirt, and Bermuda shorts and sandals. He would win, and buy everyone drinks, and sometimes he would bring a lady with him, and buy her dinner. And when he lost, he would stand by the rail, spindling his program into a hard weapon, and then tap the rail with it, *tap-tap-tap*. Like he was waiting for things to change. I'd watch Renaldo and others, like the security guard, Langston, in his crisp blue uniform. He had a thing for Maggie, the girl who sold tickets and handed out little American flags at the front. Langston was ripped — big, tight muscles that stretched against his blue cotton shirt. Always had a smile on his face, even when he was throwing out an unruly customer. And Jennifer behind the counter, who served up roast beef sandwiches and thick potato wedges. Jennifer had come all the way from Washington State to be in

Tampa, 'to be in a place where the sun shines all the time.' And my best buddy, Jake, who spent time on the streets of San Diego. An uncle sent him to Florida to work on a cousin's fishing boat, paid for Jake's trip on a Greyhound bus. Jake worked part of the time at the track, part of the time on the boat. Eventually he bought his own boat. All of these people were in transition. Even as they stayed in one place, they were still changing, the world was changing around them, and around me."

"Why did you come back?" Danny asked.

"There was no 'back' to come to, really." Jack sat down in a swivel chair and rested his elbow on the desk. "I was going there to get away from a tough situation at home. I worked hard and saved money, and even though there are temptations to spend it everywhere, I scraped my money together then moved north, went to college, and studied advertising. It was looking at these people, *good people* they were too, but seeing a bit of me in them, and knowing that at some point the race is finished, and where do you go from there? After a while, I knew it was time for me to leave."

His father paused. "You seem edgy, Danny. Everything ok?"

"I just don't know what I have to feel proud of. I just scuffle along every day and it seems like there's nothing … nothing to hold onto. Sometimes it feels like there's something but…nope, just emptiness. What can I accomplish? What have I done that's so great?"

"Every day we have to try to find things that will make us better people. There's nothing heroic about it. Little things. Sometimes we do things that we don't know will help others, but they do, and in doing those things, we become better people. I can tell you from my own experience: failure is a great teacher, but sometimes a painful one too."

Danny looked at his father's desk, which was covered with papers and nicknacks. It looked like his father's whole life was laid out on the desk; one long, tough lesson about messing up.

Jack paused, and said, "Danny, there are people, in our family even, who have done things that defined them as brave, but at the time, they didn't think they were doing anything special." He opened a drawer and pulled out a file folder, rifled through some papers, and handed Danny a photocopy of a letter.

"This letter's really old, that's why I have a copy of it. The original is with a cousin of yours. Your great-grandfather, Martin, who fought in the First World War, wrote it." Danny liked hearing stories about him. He was learning about the war in school. "Martin came to Canada from England, though his own father was originally from Belgium, and his father before him from Spain. Martin brought his wife Alice and one child with him. He worked as a labourer. By the time the war broke out, he was already close to middle age. He didn't have to go to war, but he did because he thought it was the right thing to do. He served as a private for a year in some of the worst battles in the war, in a place called Ypres, Belgium."

Danny looked at the letter. At the top was the YMCA logo, and under it was written "Canadian War Contingent

Association." His father opened another drawer, and pulled out a small cotton bag. "Have a look at these. I was hoping to pass these on to you sometime and this seems like the right time to do it." Out came a military dog tag that was designed to fit around a person's wrist; it was made of aluminum or stainless steel, and was shiny and silver. On the front of it was engraved his grandfather's name and underneath "2nd Battalion Can." Martin's number was in the middle: 454020. Also in the bag was a round gold-coloured medal with the words: "The Great War for Civilisation" carved on it. There was also a heavy brass medal shaped like a cross, with a purple ribbon. He held it up. The letters *G* and *R* were embossed in the centre of the corss in fancy lettering, and the cross' arms had maple leaves on them.

He opened the letter. It was written in neat script, carefully penned but looking like it might have been done in a hurry.

> 1st Division
> Convalescent Hospital In the Field
> June 15, 1916
>
> My Dear Wife:
>
> Just a note to you and children hoping that it finds you well as I am feeling a bit better myself. This is the first time I have written to you in a green envelope.

Danny looked at his dad, who told him that the green envelopes were reserved for longer letters home and were a privilege. Usually soldiers didn't have a chance to send anything more than a postcard.

Well, Alice, I was mad to get out but I wish it was over. I got out lucky on the 26th of April when in the front line the Germans exploded a mine under us. It was awful to see my mates go up. I was to go on sentry duty at 6:30, the mine went up at 6:20, and I was about fifty yards away filling my water bottle or I would have been up in bits.

As you see I was very lucky that trip. Fifteen of us held a piece of the crater and a good supply of men feeding us with bombs. We fought the Germans out in No Man's Land throwing bombs till the dead piled up one on another. I though the bombardment that time was bad but this time June 2 was twenty times worse.

Alice I shall never forget it. We was supposed to have a rest away back but the order came to stand to. Our Battalion marched about five miles as we thought to relieve the 15th Battalion or 48th Highlanders. Right in an open field the Germans spotted us. Right in among us they sent big shells, what we call coal boxes, at the rate of fifty-eight a minute. We had orders to scatter and dig ourselves in which did not take us long. Shells were bursting all around us. We lost a lot of men in a short time.

After the bombardment was over we went to a hedge and made a big ditch six feet deep. Up to our waist (in muddy water) we stayed there three days. The third day at 4:30 myself and a chum got a direct hit on our dugout burying us right up alive. Six fellows beat it to a safe place and said leave them, they're dead. But for an officer passing by on his hands and knees we would have been left for dead.

"What happened?" Danny asked. "How did they survive?"

"The officer heard them yelling for help, and ordered the other men to dig them out."

We was took to a dressing station at night and then sent here. We got 500 German prisoners, that cheered us up some, but things are going fine on our front now. On the night of June 3 we got our dead lads and buried them but next day the shells churned them up again. One of our lads, we buried him four times.

At one time I was lying in a big shell hole and was talking to a 48th Highlander for ten minutes before I knew he was dead. It was awful but still only for this the war would not be won. I feel that pain under my heart bad now.

Danny reread that line. "Was he sick? Did he have a heart attack?"

"No, he was experiencing what was called shellshock, which we now call post-traumatic stress disorder. Soldiers suffer it from the awful things they see and experience in the war. He was feeling pain both emotionally and physically."

I got a bag hit in the knee, sent me sprawling, lost my best chum, my rifle, but picked one up. I am beginning to feel better now.

Today is Charlie's birthday. I think of him on the battlefield. If I get another green envelope I will let you know more of how we are getting on. Remember me to Richard and Norton and Dan.

I must close now for the present I remain your loving husband,

Martin.

Danny looked at Jack. "Who are Richard and Norton and Dan? And what's a bag hit?"

"Those guys were some friends of his from the neighbourhood. I don't know what a bag hit is. I've tried looking it up. Maybe it's something you can look up."

"It's funny how he can go from writing about war and then saying something that sounds so normal, like he's able to pull himself away from the war and think about his friends like they're just around the corner."

"True. That's what life is like, isn't it. We can go through some very difficult things, some personal battles, experience awful things, and yet we try to find something normal, something *ordinary*, that we can attach our lives to."

"What happened to him after the war?"

"He was discharged not long after that letter was written. He'd spent almost a year overseas, and eight months in actual battle. He received an honourable discharge; his medical report said he was being discharged for something called neurasthenia, which is what doctors used back then to explain a lot of symptoms that they didn't really understand, but which came from the stress of warfare. Now they call it shellshock and posttraumatic stress disorder. He came home and tried to get back to his life, but he wouldn't talk about the war. The horror of it was too much for him to describe again. Interesting, though, that he was able to write it down, *while it was happening*, eh? After the war was over, he shut it inside himself and locked it up tight."

THE DIARY

Diary entry for June 3:
So I went with Ben to Tim Hortons. I wanted to get a cof-
fee. To hell with Mom and Dad saying I can't have coffee. I
can't take a lot of it anyway and I have to put a lot of cream
and sugar into it, so it's not like it's an espresso or anything
like that. Ben can drink espresso. They have a new doughnut
there, too. But that's not why Ben and I go there.

The girl behind the counter is hot, maybe hotter than the
shrink's daughter. Her name is Nicole. She's in my history,
civics, and English classes. She smiled at me the other day. If
*anybody reads this — **and I mean you Susan** — I'll kill*
them. I want to ask her out. I don't know what she would
say. But she smiled at me at Tim Hortons so I talked to her.
Nothin' much, just about history class. And what happened in
the cafeteria. "Did you see that fight in the cafeteria?" I asked.
She acted sort of interested but I think she did that to indulge
me. I'm going to go back again and see if maybe I can talk to
her about something halfway intelligent. Like, "did you fin-
ish reading Hanna's Suitcase? *What did you think about it?"*
But then maybe she'll think I'm a freak or something.

Ben's cool. He doesn't talk to anybody, or say much, but then
he's still nervous cuz his English is still not okay. But he smiles at
a couple of the girls — but then that's cuz they smile at him first.

ANOTHER VISIT WITH DR. FEINMAN

"Are you still keeping a diary?" Feinman's question poked
its way into Danny's head, like a finger going into the jelly
that he felt his brain had turned into.

"Yeah, I'm keeping it. I don't know why though."

"Why? Because it's important for you to get your feelings into a form that you can control. You can control the printed word — you create the text and you can alter it. It's all yours!"

"Yeah, so what should I write about?"

"Things that you're worried about, or things that have happened that you need to think about."

"Like, the fact that I beat someone up at my old school? That I'm angry with my parents? Angry at my dad's behaviour?"

"Sure, why not? But don't just write it down, *think it down* — and think about ways that you can take that anger and make it into something good."

Danny thought for a minute. He thought about hearing some jerk at school saying something about his dad, something like, "How's that burnt-out old goddamn freak of an old man of yours, *D-minus*?" Danny wouldn't normally have reacted — for some reason it was cool to dump on parents, at least with some of the kids. But he couldn't take it. This kid had been bugging him for weeks. Some off-handed remark that Danny had made in science class, or history class, or somewhere (*I just can't remember where*) to this kid had gotten him primed for action, and his stupid scratchy voice haunted Danny in the school hallways. *It was just such a nothing comment*, Danny thought. *What was he so upset about? I can't even remember what it was that I said to him.* Anyway, whatever it was had set this kid off, and every time they passed each other, he would make a dumb, loud, dopey, stupid comment to

Danny. Finally, it had taken a comment about his Dad to really get Danny angry. The comment sliced like a burning-hot knife into Danny's conscience, a blade thrust plunged deep into him, and Danny just couldn't — he *just wouldn't* — take it. He turned and hammered his fist into the kid's nose.

Blood gushed and Danny's knuckles were crimson and wet, but the kid came back for more. Though he was a good three inches taller than Danny, he was no match for his strength. Danny slammed him against the lockers, and then brought in a left cross that sent his nose in an unnatural direction, breaking it. The kid tried a weak jab at Danny's face, and a heavy ring on his right hand had grazed Danny's cheek, but he'd run out of energy by then. Danny gave him a quick shot to the ribs — it surprised him that they were springy, like they were made of some kind of plastic — and the kid slumped to the floor. Suddenly Danny was on the floor, too: he'd been tackled and pinned by Mr. Carson, the gym teacher. Nobody messed with Carson — he was a figure to be feared and was held in awe by most of the kids, all 230 pounds of former Olympic wrestling skill and wisecracking bravado. Danny was hauled before the principal, and his parents called in. He was lucky to get away with a suspension, and he knew it. He was told he was even luckier that the kid's parents didn't press charges, that they didn't sue.

Feinman's voice invaded his head again. "You just need to keep focused."

"I'm not a bad kid," Danny said.

"No, you're not. Don't tell anyone I said this, but in a way your dad should be proud of you. You stood up for your old man, even if it meant doing something wrong."

Danny started to think about the fun times he'd had when they lived at the old house. He could do nothing wrong in those days, it seemed. Maybe it was just his age and the fact that as he got older, being young felt like a freer time, when he wasn't bothered by what other people thought of him. He just didn't care back then. Now it felt like all he worried about was other people's opinions.

Then there was the pond near the old house. It wasn't big, but it was full of great animals — bullfrogs, toads, and garter snakes, and redwing blackbirds that clung like feathered trapeze artists to the bulrushes that swayed in the summer breeze. Tadpoles squiggled their way through the shallows around the edge of the pond, which smelled of moss and earth, heat and life. Water striders skated across the surface and water bugs did a breaststroke down into its shallow depths. Blue jays careened across the pond, enacting mock aerial battles. Of all the birds at the pond, the blue jays really seemed to live just for fun.

In the evenings, raccoons visited the pond to try their sinewy hands at catching the crayfish that skittered nervously across the pond bottom. Reduced to a distant rumble, the traffic from the highway a mile away was barely audible under the rustling of leaves. Danny liked to walk among the maple and scrub trees that grew randomly around the pond. Danny's father had told him it would eventually become a meadow. "If you look at the baby trees," he'd said, waving an arm across the landscape, "they love to be close to this kind of earth. It has all kinds of nutrients in it. Eventually the trees will get closer and closer, and more plants will move in until the pond eventually disappears."

"But what will happen to the animals?"

"They'll be fine. This kind of change takes place over years. More ponds will be created and more meadows, and the animals will find places to live."

A few years ago, maybe six or seven, Danny went to the pond and decided to bring home some frogs. But he had nowhere to put them once he got home. His mother was at the neighbour's house, and both his dad and sister were out. So he filled up the tub and put the frogs in. He counted them, getting up to eighteen before their crazy-legged hopping made him lose count. They leaped about, most of them too small to get up the smooth sides of the tub, but one fair-sized bullfrog leaped all the way to the toilet bowl while Danny was out of the room. What a surprise for Dad when he looked inside! His folks didn't get mad, though. "Just kid's stuff," they said, and laughed. They still laughed about it. About how the bathroom smelled like a swamp for a couple of days, even after the tub was cleaned.

Man, I wish I could go back in time, he thought. *It was so much easier then. Everything just seemed better.*

THE ENGLISH CLASS

His first trip to the guidance counsellor at his new school started in English class. English class was the worst. Reams of stuff by dead authors that Danny didn't know and didn't care about. It would be totally awful, if not for the opportunity to see Nicole, who sat in the third row, second seat. The afternoon sun would glint off her diamond nose stud, as if beckoning Danny's attention; her black hair had purple streaks in it and her eyes were blue. No, grey, Danny decided. *Grey eyes of mystery*, he said to himself. He tried to concentrate, but how could he when she was sitting there, looking the way she did? But it was so *boring* otherwise. So when the teacher assigned an essay, Danny had to fight to dispel the boredom that crept into his bones.

The English teacher was ancient; a sonorous old bag of bones who looked *(ok, maybe it's because we had to study both Hemingway and Hermann Melville this semester)* like a whale on legs, a great blue whale with its wrinkled throat waiting to swallow a class of students reduced as krill, and who boomed out to the classroom: "Take *The Old Man and the Sea* and create a new story that touches on the sentiments expressed by Hemingway. Make us feel that we are one with the character of the old man. Be prepared to share it with the class."

Danny was less than enthusiastic about the assignment, but as he sat at his computer that night, the words started to flow. And a week later, he was the first one to present.

He cleared his throat slightly, took another glance at Nicole, and began:

> The old man sat in the stern of his sail-
> boat, straining slightly at the mainsheet
> with a knobby, arthritic hand, and hoisted

the sail. He had done it for so many years it seemed impossible to count the number of times he had been at it, so years ago he had lost count. The water was so blue it was matched only by a wealthy matron's jewels, or by the old man's eyes, which were themselves fading after years on the ocean, but in the old man's mind it was just a little bit. In his heart, he felt the strength of endurance, of surviving a hard and sometimes difficult life.

A school of fish darted underneath the boat, turning at right angles, as if directing the old man on the water. He steered the boat away from the shore, with the expertise of one who has decades of practise, listening to the skirling sound of the gulls above. The sun cast a million precious diamonds of light across the water's surface, and landed softly in the creases of the old man's face. His thin whiskers cast tiny shadows across his leathery skin. Thin cirrus clouds streaked the sky, and the wind, well-muscled in the early hours, sought to push the boat farther on its course. All was as it should be. He cast his memory back to his wife, who had died in childbirth so many years ago, giving him his fifth child, and his only son, a son who now was many miles away. He felt a sense of peace in knowing that his life had been spent doing what he knew, not trying to achieve someone else's goal. But his peace was broken by the sound of engines and the evil smell of petroleum. He was surrounded by roaring engines and by the yelling, jeering, and taunting of a pack of young men, five of them, on Jet Skis. They raced around the small sailboat.

"Go back, old man!" they cried. "Get the hell out of our water!"

Whose water? the old man thought to himself, but didn't want to argue. The water was churning with the movement of the Jet Skis, and it was all the old man could do to keep the sailboat stable. But it was not the time to argue with young men. He looked at the shoreline, a thin line of darkened sand, and at the tiny, dark square near the coconut grove, now barely discernable, that was his hacienda. And yet, here on the water, he still felt as close to home as if he were sitting by the wood stove, reading his sport fishing magazines, and wondering how his grandchildren were doing.

The young men were hostile … crazy, he thought. Maybe they were drug runners. Or maybe they were just looking for trouble. Was it too much to ask them to leave an old man alone? The look on their faces sent his memory back to the time when he worked on a much larger boat. That was a time when there was money to be made and the ocean was like a giving mother who would not let her children down, when on a troublesome day when the sky was moody, his fishing net was torn by a thrashing, angry shark. It had soulless, cold, dark eyes, a cutting dorsal fin, and finely serrated teeth. Despite its efforts to break away, and his efforts to try and release it, it died in the net anyway. *Such a waste*, the old man thought, looking at the dead shark. Another of God's creatures, gone. He remembered the look in the shark's eye as he worked to haul it on board. *His spirit is gone*, the old man thought.

His reverie was broken by the engines roaring. One young man threw something at him. It was sparking orange flames: an empty soda bottle filled with gasoline, a rag stuck in the opening and set alight. He saw the Pepsi logo and a red, white, and blue ball on the label. The bottle clanked about the cockpit of the sailboat, bouncing around as if possessed by the Devil himself. The old man deftly grabbed at the bottle, his seasoned hands giving themselves over to the years of gripping the slippery tail fins of the day's catch. He tossed the bottle far out into the water, saving his boat from nothing more than a slight charring. But the young men were not around to see his minor heroics, having roared off down the shoreline.

Each day they came back, each day trying to roil the waters around the old man. A week went by, then two. By then, the old man knew the young hooligans' pattern. He knew the way they moved their infernal machines, and the directness of their path. So, the old man crafted a plan.

On the Monday of the third week, the old man went out again, but he kept closer to the shore. He expertly weaved his way offshore, neatly tacking his sailboat, keeping one wizened blue eye over his shoulder as the sun continued to cast its immortal light upon the waters. Then came the roar and the nostril-burning scent of marine fuel. The young men, whoop-whooping and revving their engines, roared at him across the water, as though they'd morphed into a strange combination of man and machine. They were coming at him, relentlessly, across the water, and he could see that this time they weren't out to tease or annoy him, but to defeat him. But he was undaunted. He turned toward them, gently raising himself in the cockpit of the sailboat until he was standing, taunting them.

"Bring it," he said quietly, as much to himself as to them. One rider raised something. There was a crack, a small explosion, and the old man felt a bullet tear into his shoulder, hot lead searing his flesh. No matter — he'd taken a bullet before. *No more than a flesh wound*, he thought, though a thin line of blood trickled from the spot where the bullet had torn through the shoulder muscle. Then, as suddenly as they came near, charging and yelling and bellowing, angry young bulls that they were, the commotion stopped and the five Jet Skis were suddenly riderless, their wakes causing the sailboat to bob slightly up and down as they harmlessly glided by. The surface of the water ran red with the blood of the young men. Their heads were neatly lopped off below the chin, all five bobbing in the water like corks; their bodies, arms out to the sides, were doing the dead man's float, and drifted silently on the waves. Soon the waters churned again, but this time with the movement of a nearby school of hammerhead sharks, hungry and looking for an easy meal. This was the easiest of all. The old man knew the hammerheads would come; he knew they would enjoy a good feed. Nothing would be left of these hooligans, he thought, and he allowed a small smile to crease the sun-burnished surface of his face.

What no one knew — and no one found out — was that the old man, in the dark of night and guided only by the stars, had driven stakes into the ocean bed offshore the previous night; thin poles that poked just above the surface of the water. It had been hard to do it, but he knew where to find the equipment to get the job done. To these poles he had strung taut razor wire, borrowed on permanent loan from a local prison, from skinny pole to skinny pole. Neither the poles, nor the wire, could be seen by the troublemakers until it was far, far too late. The Jet Skis would be found, he knew, at some point, and when the polícias showed up, he would just scratch his head. "I have been away," he would say. "I have been visiting my son in São Paolo. Do you know that town?"

The class clapped. A couple of people cheered. Nicole stared at Danny with an inquiring glance. And the wrinkled whale of a teacher craned his head and set a beady eye on Danny as he made his way back to his seat. "See me after class," he said, his whale noise a thin piping hiss, like he was expelling air through an invisible blowhole.

The guidance counsellor, a serene woman named Mrs. Rowcliffe, clad in jeans and a cotton shirt, a faded hippie from another era, smiled, even when telling Danny that he seemed "troubled."

"And yet, Danny, I personally didn't see *anything wrong* with your story. I thought it had impact." She emphasized the last word. "*Impact.*"

"Well, that's what I was aiming for," Danny replied with a sigh. He knew Mrs. Rowcliffe would call his parents, but he also knew that they were more than likely to give him credit for being, in his mother's words, "at least *somewhat* creative."

As he was leaving the guidance counsellor's office he reached into his back pocket to check for his house key and found a scrap of paper, a note. In neat script, in purple ink, it read, "You are a troubled and strange person." There was that word again — *troubled* — but this time it didn't seem so bad. The note finished with,

"I think you are different, deep, and *wonderful*." It was unsigned but there was a heart at the end, carefully filled in, in purple: ♥

He knew, somehow, it had to be from Nicole. In the rush between classes, she must have slipped it into his pocket. *Wonderful*. He'd never heard that from anyone before.

As he had expected, Danny was told, first by the guidance counsellor, and then by Dr. Feinman, that community service would be a "good thing" to do. Mrs. Rowcliffe had practically put him to sleep with her lecture, but something she said struck a chord.

"Have you ever heard of someone named Dale Carnegie?" she asked.

"Who is *she*?" Danny said. The only Dale he knew was a distant cousin of his mother who lived in Moose Jaw. And *that* Dale was a woman. Mrs. Rowcliffe gave him a strange look.

"Dale Carnegie was a *he*. He once said, 'When life gives you lemons, make lemonade.' In other words, make the best of a difficult situation. He wrote a book called *How to Win Friends and Influence People*." She passed Danny a soft cover book. A bland-looking man wearing glasses, his arms crossed in front of his chest, peered out from a photograph on the cover. He looked like ancient history, *and lame* — Danny had little doubt about that — and *his* time, Dale Carnegie's time, was obviously some big, long gap of time before even Danny's own father was born. Maybe his grandfather knew who this guy was. But still, Danny liked the sound of the quote. "You can hang onto this," the guidance counsellor said.

Danny took the book home and read a big chunk of it that night. He liked another quote in it: "If you believe in what you are doing, then let nothing hold you up in your work. Much of the best work of the world has been done against seeming impossibilities. The thing is to get the work done." Suddenly the bland man seemed to be making sense. He worked his way through a few more chapters.

Get the work done.

The next day, Danny went over to the church. Long Shot padded along beside him. Father Rivera was outside, surveying the fenced-in area that was going to be used by the children in the church daycare very soon. The playground was an expanse of grass and sand. Thick wooden timbers anchored in concrete poked out from the ground in what at first appeared to be a haphazard fashion.

"Hullo, Danny," the padre said and gave him a big smile. "What can I do for you today?"

"I'd like to know if there's anything that I can do for you, actually. You know, help out around here a bit."

Father Rivera's eyes glinted and his thick black eyebrows popped up. "Your timing couldn't be better!" He swept an arm towards a pile of cardboard boxes that were stacked neatly alongside the red brick church. "I need someone who can put together some playground equipment. Mr. Romeo donated his time and some of the materials, and was able to get the timbers set in concrete last weekend, but he didn't have the time to put the equipment up. If you're willing to do it, I've got all the tools." Danny remembered that his father had mentioned that there were plans to get the playground equipment up, but that Sal Romeo would be doing it. He figured he could handle it, though. With that, Father Rivera hustled into a storage shed just inside the building and came back with a big red toolbox.

"Everything's in here," he said, and paused. "You *do* know how to use power tools, eh?" He gave him an inquiring look.

"*Of course*," Danny said, hoping his little fib wouldn't be noticed. "Not a problem. However, I work best with a plan. Are there instructions to go with the equipment?"

"No problem, everything's in the boxes. Mr. Romeo marked all of the timbers to indicate which parts of the equipment are attached to each timber. Box A, B, C, etc. You shouldn't have a problem with this at all."

"One more question, Father. Can I let Long Shot run around inside here? She won't get into any trouble."

"Absolutely," smiled the priest, kneeling and massaging the dog's ears. "She's a real beauty." He went inside and Danny surveyed the boxes. He laughed to himself as he saw "S. Romeo" on the box. *Wherefore art thou, Romeo?* he thought, then remembered that the priest had pronounced it "Roe-*may*-o." It was still funny, though.

He began putting pieces of the equipment neatly on the ground. *One step at a time*, he said to himself. He opened the first box and metal pieces and a sealed bag of nuts and bolts clattered out. Along with it came a sheet of instructions. *Just follow each step, one step at a time.* He remembered the Dale Carnegie quote. "Much of the best work of the world has been done against seeming impossibilities." This would not be impossible, he hoped.

He worked for two and a half hours, drilling, measuring, and hammering things into place. By the end of this first day he had put the first stand-up pod together — the pod looked like a small clubhouse perched on top of the timbers, and he had assembled and attached a bright yellow slide to it. He came back the next day and added monkey bars and swings. By the third day he had put up the second standing pod, and assembled and attached a hanging bridge that connected one pod to the other. On the fourth day he added ladders and a rope swing to the equipment.

Each day, Long Shot accompanied him. She'd sniff around the playground perimeter, play with a chew toy Danny brought along, and then settle down in the shade for a nap. When Danny was done, Father Rivera came out to take a long, careful look at the colourful combination of wood, metal, and shiny plastic.

"By golly, Danny, you did a wonderful job. Your parents will be proud of you."

"If it's all the same to you, Father, please don't mention this to my folks. I just wanted to do something, *make something*, you know? I just wanted to be helpful."

"Well, my son, this is a great help to the church and the daycare. The little children will really enjoy it. You've done a wonderful job." He offered Danny a firm handshake. Danny winced slightly — the priest was stronger than he looked — and Danny's muscles felt a satisfying fatigue.

BEN'S PRESENTATION

Ben stood stock still at the front of the class. If he looked nervous, it was because he was nervous. He began haltingly, his voice a low, hollow whistle; it sounded like air being blown through the neck of a soda bottle.

Everybody had to do this assignment, Danny thought. *It's only eight minutes. Come on, Ben.* His friend had worried about the assignment for weeks. The civics teacher, Mr. Townend, had been kind about it, but clear: "Tell the class something about your life. Tell them something about your family history. Relate the story in a way that people will be able to identify in some way with your experience."

Danny had stumbled through his the day before, talking about judo — not very convincingly — and how it was about standing up for yourself, being focused, and taking charge. He meant it as a metaphor for his life. People had listened politely, and he hoped that Nicole, who sat at the back of the class, would like it, but she really didn't seem to have paid much attention.

"I come from a country in Africa called Sudan. The region I come from is called Darfur, which is in the western part of the country. It is a different culture there to here, but we do have some similar beliefs. We believe in the importance of family and treating your friends with respect. I would play with my friends in the village. My father was a farmer and tended cattle and goats and grew millet and sorghum. Millet is a seed and if you own a budgie or a canary you might even buy millet to feed your bird. We also ate nuts and okra and tomatoes. It is dry in

Darfur, most of the time, except during the summer. Then it rains and in places where it was dusty and dry, things suddenly become green, and lots of things grow.

"My family lived a good life. I had three sisters and four brothers. We have bigger families in Darfur than you do here, but that is what is normal there. I would play with my friends and we would go to school, which was about two kilometres from where we lived. Everything we did for fun, we did outdoors. Everything was quiet and peaceful. I would watch my mother grinding grain and preparing food for us. She would tell us stories about our family, going back many years." Ben paused, and no one in the room looked away. No one giggled. No one was even drawing idly doodles to pass the time. They were transfixed by Ben. His voice became stronger. He straightened slightly, seeming to add another two inches to his already impressive height. Mr. Townend looked downright tiny sitting at his desk, looking up at Ben.

"Then the janjaweed came. They came on horses and with guns, into our village, shooting the men and sometimes the women. There might have been thirty or thirty-five of them. The sound of the horses coming frightened us, because we were not used to the sound. The sound of their hooves pounding against the earth was like drumbeats coming from a long distance away. They charged into our village and killed two of my older brothers and grabbed my sister, who was thirteen at the time, and rode off with her. My mother was shot several times and lay gasping for breath. Then she stopped breathing. There was blood on her white dress. My father's body was found behind one of the huts. He was also dead. I cried, then screamed, then it was like I had no feeling anymore. Things just stopped inside of me. I began to run. Then the janjaweed captured me and made me work as a slave."

Ben told the story of how he was taken to a farm far away, where he was forced to work and live. The farmer was cruel and yelled at him, sometimes kicking him, but not so hard that he would injure his slave. Ben slept in a corner of a small tool shed, with a ragged blanket that was so short it didn't cover his legs. He lived that way for more than a year, and learned Arabic to survive. He was kicked and beaten by the farmer, and kicked and beaten by the children of the family. Then there was his escape, along a dirt road, running at full tilt, never looking back, but half expecting at any time to hear the pounding of horse's hooves on the packed earth, feel a hard hand on his shoulder, stopping him from reaching freedom. But he managed to find his way to a bigger road, and then joined others "displaced persons," as they were called, and made his way to a refugee camp. Life in the refugee camp was difficult too. "At the refugee camp, we waited to see if there would be food. It was about living one day at a time."

There were sniffles in the classroom. One girl in the third row sobbed.

Ben reached behind Mr. Townend's desk and brought out photographs he'd had enlarged and pasted onto boards. "Here are some pictures that show the destruction of the villages, just like mine, in Darfur. These were taken by an agency from this country that tries to help our people."

There were pictures of dead villagers and scorched huts, of refugee camps with hundreds of people gathered in small groups, the aid agency workers walking among them. "I was lucky to be sponsored by someone from one of the agencies that came to help. They gave me a chance to come to school here. And I take it as my responsibility to tell people what happened, and to try to go back someday to help my people. To find my sister who disappeared, but I don't know if I will ever be able to.

"People have to know what is happening in Darfur. There has been too much suffering in my country. It needs to be made … right. To have a chance to heal."

The students gave Ben a standing ovation. "All right, all right, settle down" said Mr. Townend, restoring order. "That was a very moving presentation, Ben. Let's open the floor to questions." It seemed as though everybody had a question to ask, and Ben tried his best to answer them all.

JULY

THE MAN ARRIVED in a small car, a lime-green hybrid. It hummed as it pulled into the driveway, then went silent as the driver turned off the engine. Danny was cutting the front lawn with the push mower. It wasn't a big lawn and his father was trying to conserve energy, so he'd paid $99 for a push mower from the Home Depot down the street. It made a neat, snip-snip-snipping, swish-swish-swishing sound as Danny pushed it across the grass, so that he felt like the barber for a green-headed monster, *snip-snipping* away at the mass of green hair.

Danny had been expecting the man, but not that he'd drive up in a hybrid car. Danny thought that he'd arrive in a big gas-guzzler, maybe some kind of SUV with long cattle horns on the front. The man looked the part of a racing man, a gambler, dressed in a cream-coloured suit with such sharp creases in the pant legs they looked like they could cut through a tin can, like the commercials for the Ginsu knives on television. He had a bolo tie pulled around a checked dress shirt and his jacket was open to reveal a rounded but tight belly. The man was built like an old football player, with broad shoulders and a nose that looked like someone had pushed a wad of putty across his face. He rose from the car slowly, easing the cramps out of his aging knees.

"Dave Langley," he said strongly, putting out a hand. His hands were leathery, but his grip gentle. "You must be Danny." His face was ruddy and he looked like he spent too much time in the sun, but when he stepped out of the car Danny had felt a blast of cold air that chased away the summer heat. The cowboy hat on his head was tilted back to reveal a broad forehead, and his dark eyes caught the sunlight, glinting like he had a secret.

Jack opened the front door. "Dave!" he called. "Good to see you."

They looked ridiculous: this bear of a man and Jack, skinny and tall, looking like he should be on a hippie commune, greying hair tied in a ponytail, Bermuda shorts, and sandals. He had a bruised toenail; it was ugly and purple in the bright sunlight.

"Why you old son of a gun." Dave rattled the words out quickly, making Danny think of cactus, mirages, and rattlesnakes. The words buzzed from Langley's lips. "Good to see you again!"

The two men went inside. Danny went around back to check his tomato plants, carefully pinching away new leaflets. The tomato plants' yellow flowers — at least some of them, it was still early in the season — were starting to bulge with small globs of green fruit beneath them. A honeybee, ignoring Danny, buzzed past. Danny could see, through the kitchen window, the figures of the two men sitting at the table, his father with a cup of coffee, Langley with a can of iced tea. Every once in a while they would laugh, his dad's laugh was light, Langley's the full-blast belly laugh of a man who didn't seem to take life too seriously. Jack had told Danny that he and Dave Langley had done business together years before: they had served for a year together in a resettlement program for refugees in Central America. Despite his appearance, Langley had a caring heart.

Danny went back around to the front and finished cutting the grass, then sat on the front stoop with a can of Orange Crush. A half hour later the two men came to the front door.

"See you soon, Dave. Thanks for coming by."

"Good to see you again. We'll see you again in a couple of months." The hybrid hummed and pulled away.

At dinner that night Jack told the news of Dave Langley's visit. Rosemary sat beside a stack of reports — she intended to eat dinner, then move to the enclosed veranda at the back of the house, sit in the big wicker chair with the purple cushions, sip iced tea, and finish her reports. *Mom never seems to get flustered by things*, Danny thought. *Even when Dad's drinking was at its worst, she just sits like a raven-haired Buddha-woman, listening and never shutting people out.*

"As you know," Jack said, and spread his hands out on the tablecloth, as was his habit when discussing important issues, "Dave Langley has interests in a variety of areas — advertising, environmental technologies, and racing. He tells me that our Long Shot is a former champ, in fact, one of the best racing greyhounds *ever*." He paused after the *ever* for effect. "He has set up a match race that would bring together Long Shot and the top dogs of the last five years. He's going to pay us $10,000 to run Long Shot — no tricks, nothing. Just the money and Long Shot runs."

Rosemary stirred, put down her bowl of greens; she adjusted her glasses, fidgeted with her watch (a regular habit she'd developed), and said, "But Jack, Long Shot is almost six years old. Isn't she too old to run?"

"I can see she still has it in her." Long Shot, hearing her name, raised her head. She was sprawled out on her cushion by the brown sofa in the living room. "I've already told Dave yes. We could use the money."

Rosemary knew she didn't stand a chance arguing the point. "I just hope she's up to it," she said, and adjusted her glasses again before picking up her bowl of greens.

THE DIARY

Diary Entry for July 3:
Okay, so here it is. I don't like writing about myself. I think this exercise is silly. I was told to just let the thoughts spill out of me like I was a bucket. Spill bucket, fill again, and spill.

My strengths: I am good at judo. I am good at writing, but I don't like it. I have a good memory when it comes to geography and history. I am a slow runner (a runner like

Ben can leave me in the dust!). I am lame at getting along well with other people. I have a bad temper. I hate my dad but I love him at the same time, and this confuses me. I wish I could talk to girls. Girls are a mystery to me. Haha, how dumb is that? I'm sort of surrounded by them. But Mom and Susan aren't really girls, not that way. The shrink is an okay guy but he asks a lot of questions. But then I guess that's his job. My friend Ben is what my mom calls an "old soul." I had to look that one up. It means that he has a depth of experience and wisdom that is different from his age — he has gone through things that most people our age never go through, and has survived the experiences, which gives him wisdom.

Danny looked over the page. It was getting easier. The words just seemed to spill out of him. Write without thinking of who or what you are writing about. Write from deep inside, the shrink had told him. *Yeah*, Danny thought, *this is okay.*

I guess Long Shot is cool. She's lying on my bed, and her eyes are half-closed. I wonder if she's dreaming of being back on the track. Sometimes her paws twitch a bit. I won't call her Rat Face anymore.

Sensei Bob taught me how to meditate. Why do people like Sensei Bob care about me? I've beaten up three people. I shouldn't feel proud of it, but two were bigger than me and I was glad to take them down. None of them got hurt badly. I got a black eye once. It was a purple eye, really. Blotches of purple and yellow.

I like the new place; it's not so bad. The plants I put in are getting bigger, stronger. I gave them plant food, but Mom said it wasn't really necessary. Before school ended, the girl from Tim Hortons smiled at me in class a few times. We even walked down the hall together. She asked for my phone number. Maybe she'll call me.

Ben has gone through a lot. I looked up the history of Sudan and Darfur. Ben went through hell. How many people can say they went through hell and survived? He's got a lot more courage than me, but I guess I should find a way to learn from his example. My biggest problem is just trying to ask a girl out! I can't even say her name! I'm so scared she'll say no. I just have to think about how to approach her. Maybe it's like someone said, "Just be yourself." I will try to be just myself.

Long Shot is looking up at me. She's like a mutant with mutant senses — she can sense how I am feeling. Mom is in the kitchen — maybe that's what Long hears. Maybe she figures it's time for dinner. I can hear Susan in her room, she's playing something — Avril Lavigne. I don't listen to that. Susan hates Dad, I think. Or maybe it's not Dad — maybe it's just her. Long Shot has left the room. I can hear Mom talking to her in the kitchen. "Good girl," she's saying. Long Shot is definitely crunching a Milk Bone.

Susan was at his door. "There's spoon pudding in the fridge."

"Thanks." Danny felt a rumbling in his stomach. Spoon pudding did that to him; he loved it. He'd called it spoon pudding ever since he could remember. Basically, it was instant pudding that his mom would make, whipping it up in the mixing bowl with milk and then pouring the thick chocolate mixture into cups. Sometimes she would make vanilla, sometimes strawberry. Danny and Susan would sit in front of the television and watch cartoons and eat their pudding, and it was one of the times that he remembered with a tinge of sadness and regret, because they had both gotten older and Susan had moved away from him — she didn't seem to care about him anymore. ("It's like being next to a person, but you can tell by their attitude that they're really a million miles away from you," he once told Dr. Feinman. "That's what happened to Susan." Dr. Feinman didn't disagree; instead he said the same thing happened to him and his sister. "It seems like they're gone far away, but you have to trust that they still care about you. And you'll find that when you're both adults you'll be close again. But you have to trust that it will happen.")

It was called spoon pudding because when Danny was young, he always complained that he could never find a spoon for his pudding. So, his mom had put a plastic spoon into the pudding cup in the fridge, standing up, so that he would always have it there. The name just stuck. Soon the whole family was calling it spoon pudding. Danny knew that when he opened the fridge the spoon would be there, sticking out of the chocolate pudding, and it always was.

The puddings were at the back of the fridge, and Danny had to move the milk carton and the jug of Kool-Aid to get to them.

He heard sounds in the backyard and went to the window, watching as Long Shot *roo-rooed* at the neighbour's cat, Mittens. Mittens sat passively (her tail madly twitching), on the top rail of the wooden fence, safe from Long Shot, who had given up, and sat back, giving a half-hearted *roo-roo*.

"Ha! You're not going to eat my Mittens today!" Mrs. Sharpe, Mittens's owner, said from her backyard. Danny wandered outside. He could just see Mrs. Sharpe's full, round face through the slats in the fence. Mrs. Sharpe said the same thing every time Long Shot chased after Mittens. Danny hated to think what might happen if the dog ever caught the cat, but maybe they would just yip and hiss at each other and then each would go their own way.

"That's true, Mrs. Sharpe. I think Long Shot really just wants to play with Mittens, though."

"Don't be kidding yourself, my boy. They would get along like oil and water. Cats and dogs just aren't meant to be together." She looked at Long Shot. "But maybe this dog is different." As her eyes softened, she quickly changed the subject. "Come around to the front. I want to give you something to pass along to your mother."

At the door, she gave Danny a crocheted tea cosy. Mrs. Sharpe made and sold them at a craft boutique at the farmers' market on Saturday.

"It's beautiful," Danny said, looking at the bright cheery colours. "Thank you."

School the next day was a drag. Danny's physics teacher, Mr. Fischbacher, gave him a hard time and kept him after class. The students called him "The Moist Towelette," because the pale and drawn Fischbacher was always covered in a thin layer of sweat that made his skin shine. "He looks like he's gonna end up in a pool of water on the floor," a classmate had said.

Fischbacher's hands were particularly moist, and students dreaded the possibility that the Moist One would want to shake their hands. Fischbacher had big, liquid eyes that bugged out of his head, and he seemed particularly excited by anything that disturbed his sense of order in the classroom. A student came in late? Fischbacher would sweat. A student asked to be excused to go to the washroom? Beads would appear on the teacher's upper lip. Danny was glad to get out of there.

There was a book sitting on his desk when he got home, with a note from his mom. "I thought maybe you'd remember this one," she'd written. "I found it in a box of books from our old house."

It was a kid's book called *The Man in the Tin Can Van*. Danny had loved it when he was seven or eight years old and insisted that his father read it to him before bed every night. He turned to the first page, then read through it:

There once were some people
Who lived in a land

A far away land 'midst a desert of sand
A wondrous land called the Land of Flin Flan

They were a hardworking folk
They would work and they'd plan
For a wondrous event
Called the Flin Of The Flan

A celebration it was. This Flin Of The Flan
With acrobats, jugglers and a musical band
There were flinners and flanners and food from a can
And the sweetest of sweets served fresh from the pan

But when the day for the Flin of the Flan came, they say
A whispery wind came crossing the sands
And with it brought clouds that did cover the land
In darkness they stumbled, dropping their cans and their pans
All was a mess and their plans went astray

"Oh what will we do?" cried the folks of Flin Flan
We need a plan, yes, we do need a plan
Otherwise, the Flin of the Flan will be spoiled
And wasted will be all of our work, sweat and toil

Then suddenly arrived there a man, a small man
In a wondrous sunshiny new yellow van
The van it appeared, was made from a can
A solar-powered van, planned and built by the man
And the man, well he smiled and waved from his van

And said, "My name is Stan and my dog here is Dan
And my van, it's filled up with bright orange fans."

And the pair, well they leaped from the van so they say
Striding up to the folks in a confident way
Stan said, don't you worry, good folks of Flin Flan
I've got a plan, yes, I've got a plan
All my fans, if you look, are powered by the sun
They've been charging for days on my cross-country run
I'll set them up, turn them on, and they'll easily push
All the sand clouds very quickly with a big *swooshy swoosh*!

The pictures in the book were pen-and-ink sketches, with splotches of yellow and orange. Danny remembered feeling sad when the man in the tin can van set up his fans and they didn't work. Somehow they were broken, jammed up. Even in their confusion, Flin Flanners ridiculed Dan, jeering him and telling him to leave.

Go away Stan, and take Dan and your fans
Pack everything up in your bright tin can van
And leave us to try and find some other plan
To drive away all of these big clouds of sand.

So Stan, having lost his confidence, left. He drove to the top of a hill and looked down at Flin Flan and the people running around aimlessly. Then Dan took a big paw and pointed out a way that Stan could fix his fans. It was simple and easy, and Stan wondered why, in his anger and shame, he didn't see it himself. So Stan set to work, got his fans working and set them up. He realized he should have never given up, and thanked Dan for pointing out the problem.

The problem, he reckoned, was not really with fans
But in the sadness and shame of the man in the van
So he tossed out his anger, and grabbed tools and spanners
And set down to work to unjam those fan-fanners

Stan returned and set up those fans
In a marvellous array
Linking them, one to the other with wiring
And pushed on a button to get all of them firing
With a whirr and a click and chug-chug-a-wheee
The fans started whooshing the sand clouds away
The darkness was gone, and the folks cheered with glee

They looked up to the hill, and they cheered Stan and Dan
Saying "Come down, please come down, and you'll be our guest
For a celebration of Flinning and Flanning at its best!"
Well, Stan stayed a while and accepted their thanks
Then packed up his things and gave his can van two cranks
And with Dan by his side, drove into the sunset
Looking for a new little town called Wa-wa-wa-wun-set
A marvellous place, near a lake really grand
And a stockpile of wonderful tin cans for vans.

Danny put down the book and closed his eyes. It made him feel good. The book reminded him of when he was much younger, wearing his pyjamas, leaning against his father on the living-room couch with a fire flickering in the fireplace, and how he always felt safe and protected, like everything would be all right.

"We need to get Long training," Jack said. He pulled at his scruff of beard, then touched the diamond stud on his left earlobe. It was one of his rituals, and sometimes he did it five times a day. "For luck," he'd say.

"Best place is a pool. The high school on Waverley Boulevard has a shallow pool, about three feet deep, just enough for Long to get in, kick around a bit, get some good exercise that won't stress her muscles." His voice was quiet, like he was planning a bank heist. Danny knew no one would let a dog use the smaller of the two high school pools — it was there for the special needs kids, the Wheelie Team, they were called — gold medal winners at the District Swim Championships the previous year.

But Danny couldn't resist the temptation to be a co-conspirator. They weren't just planning to run a dog in a race any more — they were planning something secret, something special. Long was going to be in the race of her life.

They knocked at the back door to the pool enclosure, quickly, as if they were secret agents on a mission. Mr. Jenkins, the school's custodian, answered the door. This wasn't the tired, grizzled, fat, scruffy, daytime Mr. Jenkins, his shirt spilling out of his blue pants. This was a different Mr. Jenkins, late at night. During the day he seemed slow and dimwitted, but now Danny could see that was an act. Here at eleven o'clock at night, he was bright-eyed, his face glowing. He had caught the scent of excitement, of possible danger. Or maybe he just liked the hijinks, as he called this bit of mischief.

"Come on in, come on in," he said hurriedly. "Glad you're here. I want to see how she does."

Long moved easily through the back door and into the backroom, where the pool equipment hummed.

"I've got the water warmed up nice," said Mr. Jenkins.

"Listen, Bud, you don't have to do this," Jack said to Mr. Jenkins. They saw each other rarely, since Danny's father usually took the afternoon shift at the school, after the children had gone home.

"How many laps can she do?" Jack wondered aloud. "That's the question."

Mr. Jenkins was bubbly. "The water's all ready." The pool was shallow and long enough to give the dog a good workout. Jack gently lifted Long Shot up and carried her into the pool. "Danny, go down to the other end, and called her gently. Let's see if she'll paddle her way down there."

Danny took off his socks and shoes and stood at the other end. "Come on, Long Shot, come on, girl." He was surprised at the sound of his own voice. The roughness and crackly sound was gone; he sounded confident. The dog paddled down to the end, and Danny knelt to gently pat her head.

"We've got to keep her going," Jack said. "Walk along the side and coax her back toward me." Danny walked along the edge of the pool. The water in the bigger pool sparkled in the half-light. Mr. Jenkins, careful to ensure that they wouldn't be seen, had only turned on the lights over the small pool, their glow cast wavering yellow globs of brightness across the surface. Each voice echoed. "That's a girl," Danny said. "Keep going."

When the dog was done, Danny led her up the steps at the end of the pool. She shook herself off, and allowed Jack to gently pat her dry. He looked wistful. "Reminds me of when I was in Florida."

He always got nostalgic, talking about his favourite job in Florida, looking after dogs at the Tampa Greyhound Track. "Nothing nicer," he'd told Danny. "Walking the dogs out to the track, giving the crowds a look at their favourite dog." He had put some of his wages into part ownership of a couple of greyhounds. "Good-looking dogs, but they didn't do well at the track," he'd said. But the sun and the palm trees and the finely-combed, walnut-coloured dirt of the track, the smell of the roast-beef specials in the track dining room, the little American flags they gave away at the ticket window, the regular cast of scruffy punters and track fans, the brief romance with the girl who sold souvenirs at the gift shop — all had left a lasting impression on Jack.

They took the dog back to the pool several times a week, quietly, at night, to do her laps. Each time, she got stronger. Danny thought he saw a look in her eye, an understanding that she was being asked to do something that was nearly impossible, to go against the best of the best. And somehow, he knew she would give it her best shot.

On his next visit to Dr. Feinman, Danny felt a little more relaxed, enough that he could talk a bit about going out with Nicole.

"It just happened," he said. "I didn't wait to be nervous. She was working at Tim Hortons, so I waited till she was on a break by herself, and I just went up and asked her out." He looked out the window at the traffic; it was beginning to get thick, the cars and SUVs like herd animals heading to a watering hole.

"I met Nicole at the movie theatre, and paid for her ticket. I can't remember much about the movie. It was a comedy about people running around after a bank robber who was klutzy and couldn't figure out where to hide the money he had stolen, something like that. We ate popcorn. She paid for the popcorn."

"I saw that movie. It was good." Dr. Feinman smiled a little. Danny wondered what he was thinking. "I'm glad you were able to talk to her. It wasn't so bad, then, was it?"

"Naw," Danny said, trying to be nonchalant.

Danny talked about his date with Nicole. The theatre they'd gone to was part of a new entertainment complex, with restaurants, a fitness centre, and a miniature golf course. It had rained earlier in the evening, and the air smelled of damp concrete.

"Let's be spontaneous," Nicole had said over the phone. "We'll just go, meet there, and decide." They looked at the board, all of the movies and their times.

"What do you like?" Danny had asked.

"It doesn't matter, I'll watch anything." She had impulsively linked her arm through his. She smelled of grapefruit-flavoured gum. They'd decided on a movie she wanted to see. In the theatre, Danny had listened to her talk. She talked about classes, about music, about Facebook. Nicole also said how much she liked Danny's presentation in English class. "You should have seen the teacher's face when you got to the part about the heads being cut off! I thought he was going to keel over."

Danny smiled, thinking about Nicole and how she'd held his hand as they walked home. Her palm was cool and soft. She laughed, but not too much. Everything just seemed normal and right. Nicole had seemed very much in control. Danny said so to Feinman, even while he looked down and away, avoiding eye contact. Even though he was nervous talking about Nicole, he really felt liked he needed to talk about her.

"Girls can be — and often are — just as nervous as boys when they go out on a date," the doctor said. "I know: I grew up with two sisters, and I have a teenage daughter. What it means likely is that you made Nicole feel comfortable. Just being yourself, you put her at ease. And that's a great thing for us to do for other people — give them the freedom to be themselves. So you're good for each other."

"I hope so. She's in summer school, and she asked me to go to her house to help her study for a test. I met her mom. She was very nice." There was that word again. *Nice.* Danny looked at the rubber tree in the corner of the office. It had grown taller since the first time he had been there. Outside, there was the sound of tires screeching and a horn honking. He saw three seagulls fly by the window. They moved like crazy black, white, and grey wind dancers, tilting and shifting and skating along on the strong breeze outside. Danny figured they were going to beg scraps at the hamburger joint just down the street, the place where people sat outside at picnic tables and, despite the pleading of the owner, threw bits of hamburger meat and hotdog buns to gangs of screeching, begging gulls.

"This is the way we build relationships," Dr. Feinman said. "It isn't always easy, and it's not supposed to be. We have to take away the expectations we have of other people, and let them be themselves. And it's often surprising how things just happen when we don't try to act like someone we're not, and when we don't force other people to be what they aren't." Dr. Feinman chuckled, then caught himself slightly and shifted in his chair. "But hey, I'm starting to sound like I'm *lecturing* you, and that's not what this is about, is it? We're just here to talk. And really, I'm here to listen."

Danny thought of his father. Were his expectations too high? Maybe he was expecting the worst; maybe he should just let his father be himself. He knew that, sometimes, he made his dad nervous. Maybe that's what he would do. Just be natural and maybe things would get better, bit by bit. *Life is full of maybes*, he thought.

THE RUN-UP TO THE BIG ONE

The *dojo* was quiet. The rough-textured *tatami* mats covered the entire floor. On the far wall was the photo of Jigoro Kano, the founder of judo. The picture was a washed-out black-and-white photo. His eyebrows were slightly arched, there were two creases across his forehead, like he was about to ask a question, and a thick moustache was perched over his serious mouth. His thinning hair was combed carefully across the top of his head, and his hands were hidden, possibly in the folds of the black *kimono* — or *gi* (Danny wasn't sure if it was one or the other) — that he wore. He could be anyone's grandfather, waiting for the start of a birthday party or family event. He was looking away, to Danny's right, as if gazing over Danny's shoulder at someone entering the room. It made Danny feel a little edgy. *It's almost as if the old man is watching my opponent come into the room*, he thought. *How much do I really know about Jigoro Kano?*

The facts, garnered from Googling judo websites one rainy afternoon ran through his head: he was small; he created judo in 1882; he was a teacher, and responsible for the education system in parts of Japan; he adapted judo from ju-jitsu, which was a rougher sport; he made sure that judo became part of the education system; he held himself to a high moral standard. Fight cleanly. Fight fairly. Respect your opponent.

Danny sighed. He bowed to the picture before stepping onto the mat. This would be a tough tournament, he thought.

The *dojo's* orange-and-white walls seemed to glow. Danny didn't like the walls: They reminded him of a Creamsicle, which made him think about getting sick at a county fair after eating a Creamsicle and riding the Octopus ride, around and around and around, and then throwing up white and orange on his mom's sneakers. His mom never got angry about it, though, she just cleaned it up.

He suddenly remembered a conversation with his shrink. "How do you feel, right now?" the doctor had asked. It was after Danny had finished telling him about his father's near death — of the family almost dying.

"I feel like I'm standing in a field, and it's the middle of summer and the sun is burning in the sky and everything around me, the plants, the trees — everything is growing. Other kids are running around or playing in the playground, climbing on the monkey bars, or sliding down slides. I've been here before, it's where I grew up, and I can hear the trickle of water from the creek that runs through this place. It's a conservation area. And I know it's a hot day. It's got to be 85 degrees. But I feel cold. I can't stop shivering. I'm cold and I'm alone even though there are dozens of people around me, and trees with branches that move in the breeze and dogs running around and there are butterflies. But still I'm ice cold. I can't move. I want to feel the heat of the sun but *I just can't.*" Danny had started crying; it was the first and last time he would cry at the shrink's. He hated the shrink for that, for making him cry. He was so fatherly then, he patted Danny on the knee and said it was okay to cry. *Like some scene out of a goddamn movie*, Danny thought. *All I need is for some guy in a warm fuzzy sweater to walk in the door and tell me everything's going to be okay.*

The *dojo* was filled with strong, young people. It was a monthly tournament, a tune-up for the more important, bigger tournaments to come. Danny hadn't fought in six months. He'd wondered if he could fully come back to it, if he had the drive and energy — and especially the focus — to do it. But the workouts with Sensei Bob were paying off.

Danny looked around at the other competitors. They were kids of all sizes and belt levels. Danny adjusted his green belt, whispering to himself (even in his mind he whispered to himself): *Some are bigger. Some are stronger. Some are faster. But no one is tougher.* He repeated it a few times, like his sensei had told him to.

"Repeat it, Danny, like a mantra."

Sensei Bob was about the un-toughest-looking judo master you could expect, not too tall, and not very big in the chest or shoulders. But he could move swiftly, effortlessly, sweeping the leg of his opponent quickly, tugging on the opponent's *gi*, moving smoothly to drop his adversary to the mat. Danny had learned a lot from Sensei Bob.

"Be quiet," Sensei Bob had told him earlier. He'd repeat these phrases over and over: "Be *inside yourself*. Be self-contained. Control your energy. You've got big shoulders, Danny, and a low centre of gravity. You're solid. Think of a rock. Things move *around* a rock, they don't go through the rock. Water flows around a rock. But you can be *the rock that moves*. Steady yourself, but also learn to move." He had paused and nodded towards the photo of Kano. "*Judo Ichidai* is your aim," he said, referring to the goal of pursuing the highest ideals of judo.

Danny had stood still, absorbing the words, but especially thinking about Bob's comments. *The rock that moves*. Danny wasn't absolutely sure about it, but he kind of liked it as a nickname. The Rock that Moves. The Moving Rock. Rock-moving. His mind drifted back into the competition.

Danny's first opponent was a black-haired boy from Wentworth High, he was taller than Danny by a few inches and whippet lean. He smirked at Danny. *Some are bigger. Some are stronger. Some are faster. But no one is tougher.* Danny ran the words through his head. *I am the Rock that Moves.*

They came to the mat, established themselves on opposite sides, and moved up to the tape that marked their respective starting positions; they bowed once, and then bowed again.

"*Hajime!*" the referee called out to start the match.

The tall kid came in strong, yanking at Danny to pull him off balance. Danny stayed weighted, turned slightly, then stepped neatly in, turning and lifting, then bringing his leg in to get the tall kid off balance. *Some tougher. Some bigger. But stronger. Faster.* The words ran through Danny's mind. He turned again, bringing his opponent down. The referee lifted his hand.

"*Ippon!*" he cried, calling for a full point to Danny. Danny had won.

He moved through three other opponents, winning all three. He had never come to a tournament and won every match. *Maybe this is a sign*, he thought.

Sensei Bob was busy judging competitors on another mat, but during a break he'd come over with a big grin on his face, and offered Danny a handshake and quick pat on the shoulder. "I saw you work. Great job, Danny. Big improvements. It's all about attitude."

THE DANDELION PATCH

It was a day of clear skies, with just a few horsetail clouds scattered across the sky.

Danny and Ben watched as Long Shot eased into the far turn of the track, bursting open late July dandelions. Danny felt a pang of sadness. The dandelions reminded him of a trip they had taken to the east coast: running into the surf, feeling the salt rushing into his nose, hearing the cry of seagulls. It had been a wonderful trip, a trip that you couldn't find words to describe, like a dictionary had to be invented to describe it. Building sandcastles; catching the crabs that scuttled across the shoreline; scooping up baby sea stars and putting them into little tide pools that Danny and his sister would dig out with their plastic shovels. They'd watched as the little stars unfurled their arms, moving across the bottom of the tide pool, tripping over their too-many arms like clumsy, awkward, miniature ballet dancers. There were dandelions on a patch of green lawn not far from the beach. So many that you could only see hints of green, the orange-yellow flower heads of the weeds were so densely packed. *Dad was sober that entire trip*, Danny remembered. They had played games on the beach during the day, and at night they ate lobster that they'd bought at a roadside shack and cooked in their little rented bungalow. After dinner they played Scrabble and Monopoly.

Danny could hear a voice behind him. "Aye, she's still got the legs, lads. Didn't think I'd see it, but seeing is believing." A rich, Irish brogue rolled across the field, catching Danny's ear the way a spider catches a fly. He looked again, and saw an average-sized man with the larger-than-life voice in front of the lemon yellow of the school.

The man was wearing a green jacket and khaki pants, a cloth cap was perched on his head. He walked across the field with no-nonsense, purposeful steps. Long Shot was up and trotting toward him. She was usually friendly with everyone, but she was especially so with this man.

The man stopped and, bending slightly, gently cradled the dog's head between his rough hands. "Young lady," he said, "I do believe you still have that urge to run inside of you!" The dog happily wagged her tail, nuzzling at the old man's hands. "I've got no treats for you today. But a nice try anyway."

He extended a hand to the boys. "Name's Mahoney. I come all the way up here from Florida to see how my girl was doing." He saw the quizzical look on the boys' faces. "Perhaps I should explain myself, then. I own a kennel of racing dogs. Long Shot here — do you still call her that?" Danny nodded. "Long Shot here was the best racer there was. I'd heard you might be racing her again. I come to tell you that you need to go easy on her in the training."

Mahoney launched into the story of Long Shot's life, up to the point where he had sold her. "I didn't want to sell her, you see. But I needed the money, and I was offered a considerable sum. I heard that her new owner pretty much ran her into the ground, and then adopted her out. So I was surprised to hear that she might run again. I didn't think she had it in her. But, you know, she was the best ever. A match for any dog that put its wee paws on the track."

Danny took Mahoney back to the house. He and Danny's dad grinned at each other and hugged right away. "So many years!" they each exclaimed, echoing each other. It came out, in a boisterous discussion around the kitchen table, that they knew each other from Jack's days in Florida. They couldn't believe Long Shot had brought them back together.

Mahoney stayed for a few days, sleeping on the pull-out couch in the basement. He talked continuously, but not unpleasantly, about dogs, and joined Danny and Ben for walks at the track. The amazing thing about Mahoney was that he always had a new fact about dogs, every time he spoke: he was a walking library of dog-racing knowledge.

After a few days, Mahoney took Danny and Ben and Long Shot to a place out in the country. "I've got a friend out here; she runs a few dogs."

"Name's Beverley," she said with a thin-lipped smile as she extended a handshake to the boys. She was a wizened, bony woman in her sixties. Her hands were knotted with arthritic bumps, and the sinews were taut against the surface of her skin, stretched like tight cords. She'd been seared by the sun. Her face had been toughened by decades of exposure to the weather until it looked like aged leather. But she was pretty spry. As she moved about, she reminded Danny of a cackling old crow hopping around a field.

"Bev, I've brought the best of the lot for you to see," Mahoney said.

The woman hopped about, looking at the dog. The grass on her property, which was low and set amongst rolling hills, was a light, green brown; the colour would darken from the big heat of the summer. Danny could hear barking, the distinctive sound of a greyhound's *rooing*, in the background, and saw, a hundred yards away a long, low kennel built of cinder block, with chain-link runs. Beverley touch Long Shot on the muzzle, lightly, then firmly ran her crooked, arthritic fingers down each leg.

"How's she looking, Bev?" Mahoney asked.

Danny looked across a field toward the two runs, each about fifty yards long and separated by a chain-link fence. Two lean greyhounds, each in its own run, bounded back and forth, racing each other down the length of the runs, yipping happily.

"She's fine. Just about six years old, but she probably retired at the right time. Still has strength in her legs, though." She kneeled slightly and ran her crooked fingers over Long Shot's ribs. The dog stood stock still, as if mesmerized by both the woman's voice and her strong but gentle touch.

Mahoney bragged about Long Shot's running career. "She was better than Mo Kick. Didn't earn as much, but I never saw a greyhound leap out of the gate and hold the lead better than her."

"Who was Mo Kick?" Ben asked.

"One of the best," Mahoney said. "Ran in the early 1990s. Earned over $300,000. Well, this gal didn't make me rich, but she sure didn't disappoint either."

"It's true," Bev said, straightening up after inspecting Long Shot's paws, back, and neck. "She was a grand runner, this one."

Mahoney told Bev about how he'd discovered Long Shot running around a high-school track. "Never saw anything like that before," he said. "Usually they just run away and get lost, then you find them in someone's backyard, if they ever get found." Danny shuddered.

The old woman snorted. "You don't see it too often, but this kind of thing happens. I mean, a dog that will just run a track and never wander from its owner. Takes a special kind of person, someone who connects with the dog at an emotional level." She looked at both of the boys. "Could be one of you, or both of you, I don't know." She looked into Danny's eyes. "You seem to really care for this old pup, don't you? I think she feels that in you. She must love you a whole heap, young man, even look at the way she stands by you now."

Danny was speechless. He hadn't noticed, but the dog was just sitting there, looking up at him, waiting for whatever would come next.

Bev led them to the outdoor training track on her property. It was almost a quarter mile around, tighter in the middle than a regular track, "but it does the job," Beverley said.

She got out a muzzle from an equipment box, slipped it onto Long Shot's nose, then casually pulled the walkie-talkie from her belt. "Sally, can you bring out Chester and Filly?"

A few moments later, a young woman in her early twenties came with two greyhounds, one black and white, and the other a light brindle, both muzzled, on red nylon leashes. "Sally's my daughter," Beverley said by way of introduction.

The dogs were led to a starting box.

"Aye, look at our Long Shot, like she's never been away from the track," said Mahoney, watching as Long Shot began her high-stepping nervous walk. "That's her trademark, lads. She tiptoes into the chute."

The dogs were loaded into their chutes. Sally started a mechanical lure that whizzed around the inside perimeter. A bell sounded and the gates flew up. The dogs bounded out of the starting gate, pounding against the earth. This was repeated a couple more times, as the dogs went through several short training runs. At the end, both Mahoney and Beverley said it was clear that Long Shot could run again.

"And run well," Mahoney said with a smile.

Long Shot was a natural at Beverley's track, leaning into each turn on the track as if she'd never been away from racing. She went up against Big Willy, one of Bev's best runners; a wily dog, Big Willy appeared to enjoy nothing more than testing the strength of other dogs on the oval.

Danny and Ben stood at the rail, watching the clockwork precision of Long Shot's racing. Danny marvelled at how her running style seemed to change, depending on the competition. Sometimes she looked like a she belonged on the African veldt, gracefully moving over the soft dirt of the track, her feet barely leaving a mark as she touched down, then leaped forward over and over again. Other times she looked like a toy, wound up with a spring, then suddenly released to run *chocka-chocka-chocka* around the track, kicking up soil, eating up the dirt, and throwing clods of earth everywhere. And as she got closer to the finish line, she sounded like a distant, rhythmic freight train.

"Why do they have to have the muzzles on?" asked Ben. "None of them seem to be very ferocious."

"We put them on just to keep them safe," said Bev, putting her cowboy-booted foot up on a lower rail. "Sometimes, dogs being dogs, they get excited and nip at each other. This just saves some of that wear and tear, keeps them healthy so they're not distracted by anything. These guys are pounding along at forty miles an hour: they can't be thinking about nothing else other than chasing that lure. They've gotta be focused on running, and running to win." Bev climbed over the railing and went onto the track.

Ben leaned against the rail, kicking at the dirt. The three of them watched as Bev's helpers herded the dogs back to the kennel area to cool off.

"These dogs love to run, eh?" said Ben. "How did people start racing them?"

"Ah, lad, they've been racing greyhounds since ancient times, more than two-thousand years." Mahoney was clearly warming up to a topic he really enjoyed. "The Egyptians used to keep them and feed them the best of foods, and they treated them like gods. Watching greyhounds chase down game was a great sport back then. Then the Romans brought them to the British Isles, and they started a sport called coursing, where the dogs would chase after rabbits and other game across a wide-open field. It was all about letting the dog run, using its sight, instead of smell, to track the prey. As people became more concerned about animal welfare, the game animal was changed to a bag that was dragged across a field, and that's the way they do it in many places today. They actually raced greyhounds and lurchers."

"What's a lurcher?" Danny interrupted.

"A lurcher is a mixed breed. Looks a bit like a greyhound, but with frizzy hair. They're a cross of greyhound with a collie or deerhound. Anyway, one of the English queens, many years ago, was quite a fan of coursing and it became known as the 'Sport of Queens,' same way that horse racing is sometimes called the 'Sport of Kings.'

"Coursing was brought over to North America with some English immigrants in the 1800s. They was used to hunt down game for food, not just for sport. And, of course, people would breed the dogs for the type of running they wanted, and that was a really well-muscled, strong, and wiry animal that could spot its prey and run fast over short distances.

"By the early 1900s, greyhound racing became a popular sport here, with the dogs running on tracks rather than across a field, although there's still coursing in a lot of places. A good, healthy dog will run for three or four years, and they reach their prime when they're about three years old. After age five, most dogs are ready to retire.

"I started training Long Shot when she was young, only about a little older than a year. You give them a chance to run, and you give them some training, but it would be foolish to say that *you* teach the dog. Really, they already know what they want to do, they just need a little guidance." He smiled nostalgically, surveying the hillsides beyond the track. "The thing they really need to learn is how to come out of the starting box. These pups, they love to chase after things. They watch for anything that moves, and if it looks like something good to chase, then they're off, chasing after it! So it's not hard to get them interested in chasing after small stuffed animals, and then a mechanical rabbit on an electric guide rail."

"How do they know the distance to run?" Ben asked.

"You start them out on a small course, about 150 feet, or 50 meters. Then you keep increasing it until you're up to more than 1,500 feet. That's 500 meters, or half a kilometre. When a dog like Long Shot shows promise, by the time they're a year and a half, they start training with other dogs, doing practise runs with people at the rail and lots of crowd noise, which gets them used to the sound of being at a race track."

Danny watched the dogs at the track. "My dad says they need to eat a lot of protein. Is that true?"

"Absolutely," he said. Mahoney then launched into a discussion of balanced diets, carbohydrates and fats, and the fact that racing dogs are like human track and field athletes, like Olympic competitors. Everything, from proper vitamins and lots of water to plenty of raw meat and vegetables, was geared to producing a top athlete.

"You know, there are a lot of misconceptions around greyhounds," Mahoney added, showing no signs of slowing down. "Some people think kennel owners run their dogs ragged, but others think they do need to work them all the time. But what they really need is the right kind of exercise: walks in the early morning, maybe some practise runs. They get some time in a big yard, but they can't be run too hard or they'll hurt themselves. Later on in the day they'll get another walk." Mahoney went on to talk about giving the dog rubdowns and ultrasound treatments if they have mild injuries, as well as regular visits to the vet.

Mahoney looked at his watch. "In fact, right about now my son Rufus should be rubbing down a few of the dogs. They get treated like elite athletes because they are elite athletes. It's in an owner's best interest to treat his dogs with love and respect. After all, if they're earning money for their owner, he's got to take good care of them. He wants them healthy."

And with that, Mahoney walked off to a nearby shed. Ben and Danny could hear him humming to himself.

The boys turned their attention back to the track in time to see something totally unexpected happened. The dogs were running another heat. Long Shot was coming around the far turn when she suddenly went down, shoulder first into the earth. She skidded for a few feet before coming to stop. She hopped up, and limped along the rest of the track, favouring her front left paw.

Bev ran across the track; she moved more quickly than either of the boys, despite her years. "Mahoney! Long Shot's down. I need your help!" Bev called out. Mahoney came running, lifted Long Shot up, and, following Bev's directions, took her to a cinder-block building at the end of the track. He lay her down on a stainless steel table. Bev turned on a bright light overhead. The room was set up like a vet's exam room.

"I was a vet's assistant for twenty years. You learn a few things along the way." She cleaned the grit off Long Shot's paw with a spray bottle. "She's got a cut on her pad, not a big one; she must've stepped on a sharp stone that got onto the track somehow." Long whined a little, a baby whine, as Bev showed the boys the cut; it was about an inch long and very fine, like a paper cut. "Not too bad, but she'll have to be off it for awhile."

"How long do you figure?" Danny asked.

"About a week and a half, maybe two weeks," said Bev. "Cutting it close to your race, I know. But it needs to heal."

Bev washed the wound, then put some antibacterial ointment on it and wrapped it in gauze.

"Keep her off it," she said to Danny. "She needs rest. Long Shot had a long, long layoff and now that she's started running again — too quickly, to my mind — she needs to take her time getting better. She'll still have time to get ready for the race."

Back home, a few days later, they examined the paw. "It looks pretty raw," Danny said.

Rosemary, Danny, and Mahoney were sitting at an old picnic table in the backyard. The tomato plants were growing like weeds and cucumbers had started sprouting on the vines. Danny was working hard to tie the vines off. Bell peppers sprouted from the pepper plants, and the heads of the onions were pushing at the earth.

Mahoney sipped a mug of tea, leaning forward to rest his elbows on the picnic table. Rosemary watched as Mahoney gently put the mug on the table. Danny didn't think his mother liked Mahoney. *Maybe she thinks he's sneaky*, he thought, *or maybe it's because he knew Dad from before they met.*

"It's gonna be okay, I think," Mahoney said, beckoning the dog to him. Long Shot lifted herself off the patch of thick grass she had been lolling about on. There was no trace of a limp as she trotted to the old man. "I brought something along that might help," Mahoney said. He looked at her paw, ever so gently pushing at the leathery pad, looking for discharge. He went to his truck and came back with a leather pouch the size of a large billfold, like one used for legal papers. An unusual symbol, like endless oblong rings encircling each other, was embossed on the leather.

"What's that on the pouch?" Danny asked.

"Oh, it's a Celtic knot," he said. "My ancestors believed that these symbols offered some form of divine or spiritual protection for things. I say, why argue with it? You never know when you're going to need some kind of divine protection. Anyway, it's what's inside here that counts," he tapped on the pouch, and laid it on the tabletop to open it. Inside were small plastic bags filled with crushed spices and herbal plants. "If you can bring me a wee bit of filtered water and a spoon, I'll use this stuff to make a poultice that we'll put on Long Shot's paw. Recipe's been in my family for generations. I wasn't sure if we'd need it earlier, but it looks like it might help."

Danny did as asked, and Mahoney hummed as he went to work, adding herbs to water, stirring it until it thickened into a green mush. From one of his jacket pockets he produced a gauze bandage and white tape. "Come here, girl," he said, and then proceeded to expertly apply the green paste to Long Shot's paw, wrapped it in gauze, and taped it in place.

Mahoney had another surprise for them. "You ever see booties for dogs?" he said and pulled out a leather boot, just the right size for Long Shot, slipped it over her paw, and laced it up. "She'll get along fine with this. I'll change the poultice every day and in about five days, she should be good as new." He paused. "I can't guarantee it, you know, but she should be all right to run again."

Mahoney was as good as his word. Every day he changed the dressing, and in five days, Long Shot's paw was healed nicely.

"I don't know what's in that stuff you brought, Mr. Mahoney, but it sure worked," Danny said.

"Ah, we'll know for sure, lad, when she gets back to the track, and we best be getting a move on. The race is coming up soon. This old gal needs to get her legs back."

A few days later they were back at the track, with Long Shot in tow.

"Our gal will want to run, lad, but we'll have to ease her into it."

Mahoney started giving Danny more advice about greyhounds: he could talk about them all day. Danny wondered if, in his sleep, Mahoney talked about greyhounds all night, too.

"You might've seen that when Long Shot gets nervous, or if there's something that's too new to her, she'll suddenly stand still. The dogs, they get like a statue, not moving a muscle, tensing up, ready to run."

"Yeah, I've seen that," Danny nodded. "But other times it's like she's going to take off, just run away."

"Aye, it's their nature: they go from a standstill into a flat-out run in an instant. That's why you have to have a firm hold of the leash when you're walking her. I had one red brindle that once heard a truck backfire. Didn't bother any of the other dogs, seeing as how we were near a highway and they were used to the sound of traffic. But this red brindle, Sheba was her name, up and scaled a high fence. We found her miles away."

He cleared his throat. "For racing, you have to take advantage of the dog's ability to react. And how much they love to run."

They looked out at the track. Mahoney cleared his throat before continuing, "But I have to tell you something, Danny. I have to go back to look after my business. My son Rufus needs me there. I'm going to tell you what you need to do to get her ready. Remember that greyhounds want to run that more than anything, but Long Shot still needs to be eased back into racing life. My question is, she knows what to do and how to do it, and she can do it, but are you up to it?"

Danny looked down at the dog. He thought about how happy his father had been when he'd learned about the big prize at the end of the race. "Definitely," he said. "Just show me what to do, and I'll do it."

With that, Mahoney took out a pocket-sized chart, and spent the next half-hour explaining the details of training and conditioning Long Shot.

After that, Danny took charge around the house. Getting Long Shot ready for the race would be his job. He walked her for half a mile in the morning and again at night. He prepared her food: chunks of beef from the local butcher, rice, carrots, and other vegetables, cooked in a big pot on the stove. He began cutting lawns for some of the neighbours, putting the money into the vitamins and food Long Shot needed so she'd have as much energy as possible for the big race.

That night Danny dreamed of walking through woods. *There were birch trees and maples. I was alone. The ground felt soft, like marshmallows, and it was hard to put one foot ahead of the last one,* he wrote in his journal the next day. *It was in the late afternoon and there were sounds of frogs trilling and the sharp whistling song of a red-winged blackbird. I followed the sound of a blackbird, and came to a clearing where the woods spilled away to reveal a pond where tufts of bulrushes along its green-water edge moved in the afternoon breeze. Painted turtles lazed on a log in the middle of the pond and I could see minnows darting below its surface. The ground here was firmer and made for easier walking. Beyond the pond, maybe a hundred yards away, was a racetrack; I could hear*

Long Shot "roo-rooing." It was just sitting in the middle of nowhere, in this field. I went toward her sound, and there were other dogs, all yowling and howling as they lined up in the starting box at the end of the track. Mist from the pond drifted across the track. The mechanical bunny whirred past, the gates burst open, and the dogs charged down the track. Each dog had a monkey for a jockey on its back.

The monkeys chattered and swatted at the dogs with banana peels, but the dogs didn't seem to feel a thing. Each monkey was dressed in jockey clothes, bright orange and purple and green and yellow, matching the jackets on their respective mounts. The dogs raced down and around the track, sand being kicked away by eager paws, the sound of yapping trailing away into the mist. The dogs ran into a cloud of mist and disappeared.

The mist was cold and damp and clung to my face. I could still hear the sound of dogs, but faintly. My eardrums were pounding. "Where did the dogs go?" I asked aloud, to no one. Then they reappeared on the other side of the track, coming around the final turn, heading for the finish line. And I was no longer alone, the mist lifted in a blaze of late-afternoon sun that painted the track and the sand and me in a warm orange glow. A crowd of people were lined up against the railing, ghosts of people from long ago. The announcer's voice boomed and crackled in the afternoon sun.

"And heeeeeere they come!!" Long Shot, wearing green and ridden by a capuchin monkey with a long tail curled alongside her flank, rooed and howled to the finish, coming in first. "That's a girl, Long Shot!" I called. The monkey chattered in delight. The crowds of people swept onto the track, *surrounding the dogs, stroking their tightly muscled bodies, petting the monkeys. All happy. I was elated. Long Shot trotted up to me, panting and pleased with herself.*

The dream made Danny more determined than ever to investigate the ravine that ran behind a row of houses just a few streets over. Riding by it on his bike, he was reminded of the valley that opened up behind his old backyard. "It's like a giant wedge of key lime pie, and the clouds on the horizon are the whipped cream," Jack used to say. The old ravine fell away in a mass of green and brown, down, down, down, and away from the backyard of his old house, thick and shining and filled with the woodsy smell of wild plants, dense with tangles of vines and creepers and pushing relentlessly, all the way to Myerson's Lake, getting wider as it petered out into tall brown grasses, hardscrabble earth, and lake gravel. You could hear raccoons chattering in the trees at night, the sounds of cicadas droned during hot summer days, and a lone coyote would lope through the woods long into the evenings, a grey ghost hinting at a time when woods like these were everywhere, a reminder of the time before the big housing tracts came.

There was a narrow dirt path that led through the new ravine, and Danny felt a pang of curiosity and anxiety looking at it. *What would Dad compare this to — a skinny, meandering snake that slithered its way off — somewhere?* He both did and did not want to investigate it, but the desire to wander down among the twisted trees and hanging vines won out. It was as if a hand were pushing him to find out what this place was all about. He was worried, though, that travelling through it might stir too many memories of what things were like *back then*.

Back then it was different. I didn't know what to expect in life, and so I didn't know that anything bad might happen. It seemed like things just happened the way they should. Now, things seem to happen the way they shouldn't.

Still, Danny was compelled to explore it. He took Long Shot with him for support, and wandered along the dirt trail. Crickets stopped their chorus as he passed, a chipmunk and its playmate skittered across the path in front of him, and he could hear the cawing of crows somewhere beyond the trees. He paused at a tiny pond that smelled of rotting vegetation and listened to the high-pitched conversations of the leopard frogs that climbed through the cattails ringing its edge. A fat bull-frog sat in silence, watching his passage, its large yellow saucer eyes, speckled with black pepper spots, blinking once or twice. Dragonflies scouted the cattails for bugs, and, startled by Danny and Long Shot, a muskrat slipped quickly into the pond, making a soft splash as it dived under the water.

Danny let Long Shot off her leash; it was clear that Long Shot was not going to take off after anything, since she loved to be as close to Danny as possible. As he walked along the path, the dog loped up ahead, just a few steps in front of Danny, looking back every once in a while to make sure he was still there.

They passed an old shed, its ash-coloured timbers in disrepair. An ancient crippled remnant of a farm that existed in the area fifty years before. They walked by twisted trunks of willow trees and a stand of poplars; the dirt path twisted uphill and the pair reached a ridge, where a cloud of monarch butterflies hovered over a wildly over-grown plot of milkweed.

Emerald cocoons hung from the milkweed, and some butterflies were just emerging. Danny knelt down by the chrysalises, watching a damp monarch carefully emerge from its sparkling green bed, its wings like two damp pieces of paint-splotched tissue paper. It moved slowly onto the edge of its cocoon, like a novice tightrope walker. Danny watched and waited as the sun dried out the butterfly, and its wings stretched out taut and firm, ready for flight. He turned to look at the black and orange cloud of monarchs, moving like a winged orchestra to a stand of golden ragweed, landing as a group on the flowers, drawing on them for nourishment. Danny moved along the path, his movement surprising another group of butterflies, which exploded into the air in a silent burst of black and yellow and orange fireworks.

He wandered away from the ridge, following the path toward the traffic sounds that were growing louder. He soon reached the end of the ravine at a county road, a long black asphalt snake that stretched and twisted itself past fields of corn into the distance, losing itself between two hills in the distance. It was the late afternoon and the sun was a wash of crimson. Cars followed the setting sun along the ribbon of asphalt, driving faster and faster, as if escaping from something distant and menacing to the east.

AUGUST

THE RACE WAS being held at a track far from home. It took Danny and Jack two days to get to Belle River. Long Shot rode in a crate at the back of the van. It was a small town with a Walmart on the outskirts and the road from the highway, Cole Avenue, running through the centre of town crossing Centre Street, where a line of stores, a bank, and the town library told you that this was the centre of town. Nearby, there was an Esso service station, and not far away from that was a Tim Hortons, and then the town park, where a granite monument proclaimed the names of Belle River residents who had died serving in the First and Second World Wars.

"Dave Langley said the track is about ten minutes outside of town," Jack said to Danny, who was balancing a map on his knees. Long whined gently in the back.

Jack turned onto Cole Avenue, leading out of town. They passed a retirement home, an arena, and some larger houses built on a hill that cradled the road as it wound its way out of town. Soon the town was behind them and Danny could see apple orchards and green fields out of his windows. The track appeared as a streak in the distance, not far from the lake. It was a former car-racing track. A battered, weather-beaten, old grandstand, its green paint chipping and worn, was laid out alongside the track.

Dave, the big and blustery Texan, met them at the gate. "C'mon in," he said, grabbing the brim of his cowboy hat in greeting. Dozens of cars were parked neatly on the grassy field outside the track. Though the grandstand had somehow been missed, the track had been renovated. It was a neat oval of reddish-brown sand. They were testing a mechanical rabbit in the centre loop, where it was whizzing around the track. Danny could feel Long Shot, on her short leash, starting to get agitated.

"Easy, girl," he said. "You'll get your chance to run again." They moved easily through the crowd, all of the spectators seemed to recognize the fabled Long Shot. Old duffers in porkpie hats nodded in Long's direction. There was a buzz of excitement as they made their way to the far end of the track, where the dogs were kept before the race.

"Long Shot will have to provide a urine sample," said the Texan, holding out a large plastic cup. He saw Danny's look of disbelief, and said quickly, "I know you fellas play by the rules, but it's understood that we're being held to a set of rules, pretty strict ones, too, and I have to make sure we all play by them."

The dogs were led into the starting box. Most of the eight dogs were jumpy and strained a bit at their leads, but Long Shot was calm. A few minutes earlier, the announcer's voice had rung out, like thunder on a clear day: booming and powerful and commanding.

"Ladies and gentlemen, boys and girls. A special event for you today. A match race featuring the greyhound world's best of the best for the last three years."

The crowd murmured its approval. A heavyset man with an unlit cigar furiously wrote down names as the announcer's voice rolled across the weather-beaten grandstand. A woman in blue jeans and a canary yellow sweater got up from her seat and hurried to the betting window. An old man with a leathery face, his neck a length of deeply furrowed wrinkles, craned his neck to see the dogs. *He looks like a turtle*, Danny thought, *a turtle watching dogs*.

Long Shot was wearing a red jacket with the number 7 on the side.

"Lucky number," Jack said quietly. His enthusiasm, it seemed, had been tempered by seeing the other dogs at the track.

Granted, they were all around Long Shot's age, all of them great winners, but some were imposing. Bristol's Coneybeare, a tall, dark red female out of Sarasota Springs, high-stepped it past the punters along the rail. A tall, thin man in an oversized green tweed jacket leaned against the rail, pushing back the brim of his hat as he eyed Coneybeare. "This one's a winner," he said to his companion, a woman in blue jeans and a sweater with NASCAR emblazoned on it. "I'm damn sure of it."

Other dogs came onto the track. Coleman's Number One, a smaller but very wiry dog, like an oversized whippet, pranced about; a blue brindle prizefighter ready for battle. Langston's Merit, a black and white runner from Georgia with a reputation for fast starts, simply gazed at the crowd with an unsettling confidence. Then there was Finian's Rainbow, a grizzled, dark brindle veteran of more races than anyone could remember. He was likely the most muscular dog on the track, a powerhouse who had edged out some of the best runners in the United States. Danny, looking at the field of dogs, felt a sense of awe.

The mechanical rabbit hummed along, around the inside of the course. Whirring past the gate, frozen in time like a cartoon rabbit, Bugs Bunny leaping away from Elmer Fudd in still life. And yet it was moving; moving faster and faster, it seemed. The dogs, seeing it moving, were hyper-sensitized and started pushing and straining to chase after it. When it was about twenty feet past the gate, the doors swung open, and the dogs hurled themselves onto the track.

"Aaaaand, they're out of the gate!" the announcer's voice boomed. Small clods of earth were churned up as the dogs' sinewy bodies pushed them, great machines of muscle and bone and tendon, trying to move each of them further ahead of the other greyhounds in the field. Long Shot's red jacket flashed by the grandstand, like a quickly darting bird on the wing. Long was out in front, and Danny could almost hear her panting as she coiled and uncoiled her muscles, her back a solid line of animal grace and power. The next dog, Finian's Rainbow, the muscular dog with a yellow coat and number 3, pushed alongside Long Shot. Long's shoulder was hugging the rail as Finian streamed past, huffing as he strained to reach the madly, wildly fast-moving rabbit. Long was not to be outdone. Her hind legs moved in a smooth half-circle, reaching just ahead of her front paws, touching down, and then vaulting her forward. Small puffs of dirt and dust rose from the track as she moved forward, first bumping her muzzle at Finian's haunches, then coming even with the bigger dog.

But a burst of speed from Coleman's Number One sent the smaller dog hurtling forward. Panting, his chest heaving, he held the lead for a half second, then eased back, his burst of speed lost, the effort too much for him, as Langston's Merit pounded forward to pass him, reaching Long Shot's tail, then gaining enough hard fought ground to bring his muzzled nose even with Long's right shoulder. Long Shot and Finian, neck and neck, were still in front, moving slightly ahead of the pack. The finish line came into view. The lights of the track caught Long Shot's dark eyes, throwing off little sparks of glitter. The crowd began to cheer, a swelling upheaval of shouts and mindless whoops and gritty words and noise like Danny had never heard before became an ocean's rush of sound that erupted and poured out onto the track. It was as if the sound itself was pushing, nudging, and propelling the dogs to the finish line.

Go girl, go! Danny cheered to himself.

His father was pounding a rolled-up programme against his fist. "Yes! Yes!" Jack yelled.

The last twenty feet felt like slow motion for Danny, like in an action movie, for dramatic effect. Long Shot's legs appeared to turn into pistons, pushing into the earth, her nose straight ahead, the number 7 a streak of black against the red of her jacket. She leaned into the run on the least few feet of track, edging out Finian's Rainbow by a nose.

"She won! She won! Whoo-hooo!" Danny's father cheered.

The crowd erupted into an impromptu chant: "Long Shot! Long Shot! Long Shot!"

Danny ran down to the rail. "Long Shot!" he cried. The dog looked over, recognized him, and wagged her tail as she was led back to her crate.

The celebration afterwards was outstanding. A banquet was set up in a large meeting hall at the local arena, and the room's laminated wood floors were polished to a shine, the tables were laden with fried chicken, ham, roast beef, all kinds of vegetable dishes, and desserts. The dogs were kennelled in a specially built enclosure in a shady area outside and given their fill of "the best dang dog food this side of Texas," Dave Langley said with a smile. Mahoney and several others beckoned to Danny and his dad as they joined the line of hungry greyhound fans. They filled their plates and headed to the table, stopped along the way by smiling people offering their hearty congratulations on Long Shot's win. At the table Jack relaxed and basked in the adulation that continued to come, long into the evening. Three offers to purchase Long Shot were gently turned away. A small Zydeco band was set up at one end of the room, and soon people were up and dancing around the room. Even old Mahoney got up for a two-step.

SEPTEMBER

SCHOOL BEGAN WITH a slow and solemn shift from summer. Danny felt cheated being in class, given that the weather outside was still summery, sunshine buttering the grass outside with a golden glow, the sound of cicadas continuing to drone in the trees; and yet it was September and the unofficial beginning of the long slow dragged-out crawl to the end of the year.

Danny was in English class, listening to Mrs. Sharples drone on about Shakespeare and love, Romeo and the House of Capulet, and it all ran together like a cupcake that had been left out in the sun; Mrs. Sharples voice was the icing itself. Suddenly, Danny was awakened by her voice. "Danny, you need to go down to the principal's office."

The principal had a message. It was a jumble of words in the September afternoon, and the principal's voice, so different from the sugary sweetness of Mrs. Sharples' voice, was firm but kind, heavy, like a block of steel dropped on velvet.

"Danny, your father's been taken to the hospital."

The next few hours were a blur. His mother came to pick him up and take him to the hospital. At the hospital, they went to a too-clean room that reeked of disinfectant. His father lay prone, quietly; a narrow plastic tube dripped clear fluid into his right arm, near his tattoo. His earring was gone, and his long hair spilled out across the pillow. He was unconscious.

"Your father has bleeding ulcers," his mother said, before breaking into sobs. Susan stood stone-faced, looking out the window. Danny eased into a chair next to the bed and grasped his father's hand. "They tried to stop the bleeding, but they can't. He's in a coma. Your daddy is dying."

Danny felt like someone was standing on his chest. He couldn't find his breath and his head pounded.

Jack spent days slipping in and out of a deep sleep. When he was conscious, he managed to make the kind of small talk that fathers make with their sons. And, despite his illness, he could see the anxiety on Danny's face.

"Don't worry about me, Danny." His hands were still strong and the knuckles of his fingers stuck out like knobs of polished stone as he gripped Danny's hand.

One afternoon, they were alone in the room. There was a murmur of nurses outside the door. Rosemary and Susan were in the hospital cafeteria. The humming and beeping of technology, the heart-monitoring machine and other equipment was the only sound apart from their voices. A single light above the bed threw a yellow-white glow across his father's face. Sunlight peeked through a narrow window, highlighting two rows of carefully arranged get-well cards and a couple of potted plants on a table.

"Don't worry," Jack said again. "I know that doesn't make much sense, but I want you to think about what you want to do in your life. Don't mourn me. I've lived my life, Danny boy, and it's a life that I'm not always proud of, but it's there, trailing behind me like the wake of a boat on the ocean. Remember the way we looked at the boats when we were on the East Coast?" Danny nodded and his father's eyes glittered, reawakened by the memory. "Those lobster boats going out in the morning, and there was just a hint of orange sun on the horizon? The waves would drift here and there, but it was still the ocean. The things that happened to me, and the things that I made happen, are still my life. I accept full responsibility for the things I've done. I just wish I'd been a better dad. I know that seems to be something all fathers say to their sons at one time or another." Hot tears welled up in Danny's eyes.

"I can see them now," Jack said, his voice had changed and his eyes drifted. He was shifting into another reality, his mind drifting on a tide of thoughts to another place or time.

"What do you see?" Danny asked. "What are you looking at?"

"The dogs that ran at the track when I was young. We'd take the boat out in the morning, shrimping, haul-ing in nets, and then clean up and head to the track in the afternoon. I think those dogs were so nuts about me because I still smelled of shrimp. You know how they love their seafood. And there was a big dog, Bosco. He was black and had a white marking on his face, in the space between his eyes. And he was a gorgeous runner. I loved taking old Bosco to the starting box. The sun …" his voice trailed off as he slipped into a deep sleep. Danny felt the warmth of his hand and listened to his shallow, raspy breathing.

A little while later, Jack awoke.

"I brought a book to read to you," Danny said, reaching into his backpack. "Are you okay if I read some of it?"

"What book is it?" his dad asked.

The Man in the Tin Can Van."

A smile appeared on his face. Nudging the edges of his dry lips, like the little cracks that spread across ice as the spring sun warms it up. His eyelids fluttered. "I'd love to hear it."

Danny began. "There once were some people, who lived in a land. A far away land midst a desert of sand…"

As he sat next to his father, Danny could feel the afternoon sun baking the inside of the room. It was the time in the fall when warm winds seemed to suggest a return to summer, though the egg-yolk and scarlet colours of the tree leaves signalled otherwise. It wouldn't be long before cool breezes would turn to frosty winds. Danny looked at his father's half-open eyes; the whites were yellowed and marbled with streaks of red. Jack woke up, breathing heavily, and looked at him.

"What day is it?" he asked.

"Tuesday," Danny replied.

"I was dreaming about something, thinking about when I was growing up. My family had a small property on the edge of town. My father raised dogs there, a small kennel. It was something my grandfather had done for years and my father just picked up where Grandpa left off. We had three greyhounds growing up and two gun dogs, Chesapeake Bay retrievers that my father trained to retrieve ducks. He loved duck hunting. I only went with him once, when I was twelve. I was a pretty good shot, had practised on a range out behind the house — in those days, out in the fields and away from the town, nobody bothered anybody who shot target practise. I spent a lot of afternoons hitting — or trying to hit — tin cans lined up on a sawhorse, with bales of hay behind it. But I couldn't stand to kill a duck.

"I shot one, once. Watching it fall from the sky, it was like part of me being torn away. I could feel it in my heart." He reached as if to touch his heart, but his hand made only a gentle waving motion above the white sheet. "The dog, Bruno, was a big, muscular animal. Full bore, he'd throw himself into the water. Bruno lived to swim. He'd leap out of the duck boat into the water, chugging away toward the dead bird." There was a pause, and silence except for the hum of the monitors.

"But the greyhounds, those were my favourites. Toby, Gilly, and Mack. Watching them run, we took them coursing in those days, you just felt your heart leap. I'd take them out to a coursing competition and Toby (he was the fastest), Toby would go in a pack of three and take off across the course, chasing the bag, shoulders bulging and tongue hanging out. It was as if he was chasing after his own little piece of heaven.… The field was full of rises and dips, and I would stand and cheer him on as he tore away at the ground, pushing himself ahead of the others. 'Go Toby! Go Toby!' Dad was less excitable than me. He just watched and made some notes and shelled peanuts. Never said a word, just studying the dogs and eating peanuts. Gilly and Mack were good dogs, but there was no dog like old Toby."

"What happened to Toby?"

"Ah, he lived a long life. Sixteen good years. He was a stud dog and had lots of puppies. Died in his sleep. A happy life."

Danny's father died later that afternoon. He was cremated and some of his ashes were buried next to Grandpa, in a space in the cemetery near a pine tree. They saved the other part of his ashes, to scatter in Evelyn Jossa Park, where they used to walk Long Shot.

A week later Danny was sitting with the padre. The priest's office smelled of wood and cologne. "Danny, how are you feeling about your father? Do you want to talk about it?"

"There's nothing to say." Danny looked out the window.

"Okay. I have something to tell you." The padre reached into a drawer and pulled out a scrapbook. In it was a newspaper clipping. "Read this." He passed a photocopy of a newspaper clipping to Danny.

The story was short and framed a photograph of a car being pulled from a canal. It was dated before Danny could remember; he would have been about a year old.

The headline read, "Good Samaritan Saves Local Priest from Canal."

"Police are searching for a good Samaritan following the dramatic rescue of Father Alonzo Rivera from the Bradley Canal. The priest, who is pastor at St. Gabriel's Church, was driving along Canal Road late last night when he skidded on a patch of ice." There was stuff about how a man dove into the river and pulled Father Rivera from the car, then more stuff about the canal and what a dangerous road it was on. Then the last two lines: "Police are looking for a man in his mid- to late thirties, between five foot eleven and six foot two, described as having a ponytail and beard, a gold stud earring, and a thin build."

Father Rivera's eyes were moist. "He saved me that day."

"Who? God? Jesus?"

Father Rivera laughed. "No, not that *He* — I mean *your dad*. I know it was him. I panicked, trying desperately to open my car window. Then I thought I saw Jesus, the long hair, the beard, floating in the water next to my car. But Jesus didn't wear a gold earring, and he didn't have a tattoo of Chinese characters on his forearm. But he had a look of calm on his face, your father did. I don't know how he got me out; I blacked out after seeing his face. But I remember him leaning over me on dry land, and me vomiting out water. He had performed CPR and did whatever it took to save me. Then the police, the ambulance, the paramedics surrounded me. And your father was gone. I asked God to help me find him, thank him for what he did. But *he* found *me*, and I guess my way of thanking your dad was to make sure he never went without. I owe him my life."

NOVEMBER

RETURNING HOME FROM school one day, Danny was greeted by a tail-wagging Long Shot. She strode up to him in her elegant, trotting way, tongue lolling out. The smell of cinnamon tickled his nose: Rosemary was baking an apple pie.

After his dad's death, Long Shot had returned to normal pretty quickly. "Why doesn't she seem sad?" he asked his mother. "She doesn't seem to miss Dad at all."

Rosemary was writing a report; she seemed to write endless reports, filling in information in boxes, checking off details, spending time on her cellphone with clients. She pushed her glasses up her nose. Her eyes were bright, and she reminded Danny of the squirrels in the park, gathering nuts for the winter. Like them, Mom moved about her work and through the house purposefully.

"I remember a story growing up," she said as she put down her pen. "Someone, one of my aunts, I think, told me that animals don't mourn the death of people, not the way people feel sad about someone dying. They accept it as a part of their lives, and they quietly know that they too will die, and they will join the person they love again, so they don't worry about death the way we do. I'm sure Long Shot misses your dad in her own way, I think. But she knows your father's spirit is with her, even after death."

Danny paused, then gave Rosemary a hug. "Thanks, Mom," he said quietly.

He went outside to the backyard. The neighbour's cat had kittens, and they were mewing on the other side of the fence. Long Shot trotted to the fence and an inquisitive kitten batted at her nose, poking a tiny velvet paw through the fence. Despite her initial concern over dogs with cats, Mrs. Sharpe had grown to appreciate Long Shot's good nature. She had promised one of the kittens to Danny, and Rosemary was okay with it. Even though she was always gentle, she was a little easier on him these days.

Something glinted in the grass along the fence. Danny reached down and picked up a medal, with his father's name inscribed on it. The year was rubbed off, but it was a silver medal and there was the image of a swimmer, standing on the blocks, ready to leap into the water engraved on it. "2nd Place, Belleville Regional Finals." Danny wondered how it got to the backyard.

As he looked at the silver medal in his hand, something else caught the corner of Danny's eye. It was the glint of hard metal in the sunlight, just an edge poking through the earth. He put the medal in his shirt pocket, kneeled down, and pushed away the long grass. The rounded edge of the container felt like a heavy cookie tin. Danny went to the tool shed for a spade and then began carefully digging at the crumbly soil, which came away easily. He pulled up a metal box the colour of watered-down tea; its sides and lids were heavy and a Celtic knot was carved on the top, like the one on Mahoney's herb pouch. He pried open the box with the edge of the spade. Inside was a packet of news clippings and letters; they smelled musty, like an old room of library books. The clippings were yellowed with age, but not touched by mildew or mould.

Danny took the box inside the house. He carefully opened a newspaper article. "Local Sailors Rescue Shipwreck Victim in Gulf." There was a picture of his father — a much younger version — shirtless, wearing cut-off jeans, with his hair tied back in the familiar ponytail and a droopy moustache like baseball players used to wear, smiling on board a fishing boat. Beside him was a heavily built man with a set of thick black sideburns, who looked like the captain of the boat, and several other young men, all of them smiling. They were standing around a middle aged woman with a blanket over her shoulders. A slightly older man who looked vaguely familiar was in the background, holding onto a stay that was affixed to the mast. The article told how the fishing boat answered a distress call during a storm and how his father, "a former swimming champion, dove into the waters, a line attached to the belt of his dungarees, and, despite the threat of sharks in the immediate area, churned through the waves to the listing boat and rescued novice sailor Maria Martiniano before her pleasure craft was sucked beneath the swirling, choppy waves of the Gulf of Mexico."

There were other clippings. "Local Kennel's Top Dogs Big Winners at Coursing Event." "Ad Executive Gets Nod at North American Advertising and Marketing Gala." There were other stories and pictures that showed a side of his father he had never seen: a smiling young man, bright and full of life, ready to put himself in danger's way to help others, without caring that it might not be a great idea. There was a faded colour photograph of his dad on board one of the ships Greenpeace use to stop whalers from making their kills in the Pacific. His father's face was sunny and his eyes sparkled. It looked like it was late afternoon and sunlight splashed across the deck of the ship. Next to him was a man with a wild-looking beard that flew in all directions with the wind; he wore a beaded headband and a look of keen intensity. On the back of the photograph his dad had written, "Bob Hunter and me." Danny knew that Bob Hunter was one of the founders of Greenpeace.

Tucked underneath all of that was a love letter that still smelled of lemon and lilacs (*What a strange combination!* Danny thought) as if the letter had been written yesterday. But the date would have put his dad at seventeen; he figured the writer, whose name was Amy, must have been no more than sixteen. In sweet curling script with smiley faces dotting the *i*s and a thick underlining of words like *love*, the letter spoke of caring and longing and warm hugs and holding hands and walking along a beach. Danny imagined what his father must have meant to this girl when he was young, and Danny wondered what his father did, what the girl Amy did, or what both of them did, to bring their relationship to an end.

It made him wonder: Danny had always loved his father, but had got used to seeing Jack as tired, aging, his energy spent. He remembered a summer day when he was about ten, and they were driving across a stretch of county road, and the car ran out of gas, *sput-sput-sputtering* to a halt, and Danny had felt like they would be swallowed up by the heat and the harsh sun. Danny knew that Jack's alcoholism had taken a toll on his body, and sometimes he was like a car that had run out of gas, out on a lonesome highway. But then he remembered how his father had turned that day into an impromptu adventure by the side of the road, how Jack had trooped off down the highway, gas can in hand, to a service station a few kilometres away, then hitching a ride back with a chicken farmer and 500 squawking hens.

Danny paused, and a flood of memories came back, of small kindnesses and hugs and bedtime stories, walks through the park, and the spark of enthusiasm in Jack's hazel eyes. He had a depth of caring that had no limits, no bottom. And here in this metal box was evidence of a life more fully lived, of his father loving others and laughing and being a … well, a hero. He rolled the word around in his mind: *Dad was a hero, but he never talked about it.*

THE BIG TOURNAMENT

His father's death sat heavily in a corner of Danny's conscience. Now Danny was faced with tackling his own emotions and finding the courage to go to the big tournament he'd been preparing for. His father had wanted that.

"When's the tournament?" he would ask, then check the calendar. It was already written in red pen. "Can't wait to go. You're going to kick the crap out of the competition, my boy." Whenever he got excited like that, Danny noticed the creases in his face, crow's feet crinkling at the corners of his hazel eyes. It made him look older but also kind of cheerful. Danny could see, like a snapshot from the future, what his father would look like at seventy or seventy-five. But here he was, dead at sixty.

Tournament day loomed like a giant sitting on a mountain that Danny was in the shadows of. The big red-headed kid would be at this one, and Danny knew he was in for a battle.

He'd been training at home with a weight set his mother bought, and which he and his father set up in the basement. He continued with his push-ups and sit-ups. He continued running, moving to greater distances and through interval speed training. Long Shot trotted alongside him and, for her, it was just a warm-up. But he didn't take her for the flat-out runs. Now it was time for her to really enjoy her retirement.

He kicked the soccer ball around with Ben and, in the basement, Danny bench-pressed increasingly heavier weights and secretly felt good about the steely tone of his biceps.

The day of the tournament came. In the early morning, he sat in a corner of the basement and tried to meditate the way Sensei Bob had taught him. Counting his breaths, looking at a spot on the wall. Cross-legged, his hands carefully placed in an oval in front of his bellybutton, in a position Sensei Bob called the "cosmic mudra."

"Do this, and do it this way," Sensei Bob had told him weeks ago, sitting down on the *dojo* mat and instructing Danny to sit across from him. "Think only of your breathing. Think of nothing other than counting each breath. Don't try to force yourself to *not think* — just let your mind wander. Think of nothing except counting your breaths. Count your breaths up to twenty, then start over again." Sensei Bob had set a timer next to Danny, one that wouldn't tick, so there would be nothing else to focus on. "You must learn to relax. Lift your shoulders, hold them for ten seconds, and then let them sag and begin counting your breaths. Look at a point on the mat but always work to ensure that you keep your back straight." Danny had started with five minutes, then worked up to ten and then twenty.

"Meditation is a funny thing," he said to Sensei Bob later. "It's like I'm not quite going to sleep, but I'm very relaxed. I really needed the timer to make sure I didn't go overtime. Otherwise I would have lost track of time."

"That's kind of what you want to do," Sensei Bob laughed. "You want to reach a point where you lose track of everything, even yourself."

Danny's mother drove him to the tournament. There was a sea of people in the community centre, some for judo, others for a hockey tournament that was also happening there. The judo room had a crowd of competitors, all with different belts. Danny warmed up. He thought of his father.

It might be a bit cliché to dedicate the competition to his dad, but the thought skipped into his head anyway. *For Dad.*

He eyed the competition. They were all taller than him. One competitor, a rough-looking character with thick hands and a wild-looking goatee, must have weighed about 275 pounds. Because it was an open competition, he could face anybody. One boy, big and red-headed, was sneering at him. He seemed familiar, like Danny had seen him before. But he knew this kid was quite a bit older and went to a different school. *What's that guy got against me?* Danny thought.

Sensei Bob was on another mat, getting ready to judge the younger kids. He winked at Danny and gave him a thin smile. *Sensei Bob doesn't seem too worried*, Danny thought, *but then he's not going to go up against a behemoth.*

Danny said hello to the other fighters from his club, three boys and two girls; he didn't hang around with them outside of the *dojo*. He stretched some more, then sat and waited patiently for the matches to start — or as patiently as he could, for his name to be called.

His first match was against a rangy kid from the Budokan Club. Danny remembered him from a previous competition. He was a skinny kid but fast. Sensei Bob's words came to him as he looked across the mat and up at his opponent. "Never lift your arms above your shoulders. Turn, turn, the opponent, and if you're shorter, close the gap. Don't let them use their longer reach to their own advantage."

Danny handled his opponent well, pulling and shifting and moving him about the mat, hearing only the huffing of his own voice and the scuffing of bare feet. He used the *osotogari* move, sweeping his leg to the outside, then drawing his opponent over his own leg and down onto the mat. He won that match, then the next two, and then he faced the big kid with the red hair.

The kid had been furious, watching him before the match, and now that they were tangling, he was trash talking, just low enough that the referee couldn't hear. "I'm putting you down, D-minus." *Why is he calling me D-minus?* Danny wondered. Only a few people — rotten, stinking, nasty people — called him that. He spun the kid around, whacking at his ankles with his feet, then took a misstep and the kid managed to drop him to the mat, clumsily so it would take a pin for him to win. He wrapped his arm around Danny's neck. It was supposed to be a hold that would lock him down, but Danny could fell pressure.

"You're *choking me*," he managed to get out; he felt dizzy, and darting lights, like trails of tiny silver fish, swam in front of his eyes.

"You broke my brother's nose, you son of a …" Then Danny realized why this guy was so familiar. The same eyes, the same jaw line, the same angular face. It was the brother of the kid he'd beaten up in the school hallway.

"I didn't mean to hurt your brother," Danny said, knowing that the clock was ticking. They spoke in harsh, strangled whispers, Danny's mind dancing on the edge of consciousness, the big kid in a fury of uncontrolled anger, but still aware that the judge could haul him off at any time, disqualifying him.

"I don't freaking care!" he hissed. "You're gonna pay for it." Big Red was angry, tightening his grip.

Danny started feeling woozy … like maybe if he just gave up, he'd be free of this guy, free to leave and go home and forget about it. But Big Red was still fighting. "Your old man was a loser. Everybody knows that."

Danny's heart turned to stone. One word came choking its way out of his throat repeatedly. "No. No. No." He was within seconds of losing the match and, spinning madly on the floor, got the word out while trying to figure out a way out from under this guy. Sensei Bob's face floated through his thoughts. *There is a way to escape*, Sensei Bob said wordlessly.

Then, strangely and luckily, a bee began buzzing around Big Red's face. He looked away, loosening his group enough for Danny to get a knee up for leverage into Big Red's chest; then he shifted his right foot, and pushed Big Red off of him. Danny moved up quickly off the surface of the mat, scooted in, and grabbed his opponent's *gi*, then moved into his opponent's space, and executed the *yama arashi* ("You may want to call it the Mountain Storm," Sensei Bob had told him), grabbing the right sleeve of Big Red's *gi* and throwing his opponent over his hip. Sensei Bob later said that it was one of the few times he'd seen a student execute a throw like that so well.

The match was done. Danny had won.

He then faced the biggest competitor, the rough-looking guy, but lost, settling for silver.

He looked into the crowd. Mom was there. Nicole was standing by the door. She told him later that she was worried for him, scared that he might be hurt. He did have some bruises, and a red mark across his neck, it's true. "But I never felt better," he told her.

"Your dad would be proud," his mother said quietly.

MARCH

DANNY BEGAN A new page in his diary.

I miss my dad. It has been six months since he died — half a year already! I think Long Shot misses him too. She will stand near the front door, staring out through the screen door at the time that Dad would usually come home, the way she would when he was alive. Is she expecting to hear the tires on the driveway? Does she expect to see him to come through the door? Or is she just watching the neighbour's cats, or squirrels running across the lawn? Anyway, I am surprised that I have held up as well as I have. I accept the fact that Dad's gone, that there is always going to be a certain amount of sadness. But I can work through it.

What else can I write about? I promised Feinman that I would write every day, even if what I write might seem to have no meaning to me right away. Maybe someday it will. I've missed a few months, so I guess I should catch myself up so I remember things later.

I'm still talking to Dr. Feinman. I'm actually dating Nicole. I still don't get why she likes me, but maybe I have a self-esteem problem, I don't know. There's a lot I still don't know. The shrink says a lot of this is stuff I have to figure out for myself. That's my job, he says, and he's right.

Something else I didn't know before: Mom said Dad had prepared for the future by buying life insurance. He managed to keep several policies going and there was money from his old work, and Mom put the money into kind of a trust fund for Susan and me. And there's the $10,000 Dad got for running Long Shot in the big race. All of it in cash — a stack of bills held together with a thick rubber band. I had never seen a hundred dollar bill before. It didn't seem as impressive as I thought it would.

"Money is important," Dad said on more than one occasion. "But not as important as family." Anyway, a big chunk of that money already went to pay bills. But I believe Mom when she says things will be okay.

I just got my licence. Mom says I can drive the car, but she's nervous about me driving at night. I promised her I would be careful and I know she's going to hold me to it.

What else? I want to get some fuzzy dice to hang from the mirror.

I'm still kind of annoyed that Ben moved to Listowel. I miss him. His cousin from Darfur was relocated there, so that's where Ben wants to be. Apparently quite a few of his family members will be moving there. There's a factory there *that his cousin works in, and it's expanding, so there will be job opportunities for his family. Ben was happy to be going to Listowel, it was always important to him that his family was able to reunite. So I guess that's good for him.*

He wrote a poem that he called "Scattered in a New Diaspora." It was pretty good, but I had to look up the word diaspora. It means the dispersion of people from their original homeland. I'm going to remember it. I want to read more about Darfur. Family is everything, Ben told me. He was right. Before he left, he won the 400-metre final in track and field for our district, and came third in the regional finals. Hopefully I'll drive to Listowel sometime to visit, and maybe I can take Nicole. It will be a long drive, but worth it. We'll drive around Listowel with Ben and see the sights.

Danny turned to look at Long Shot, lying on her back, paws tilted at all angles in the air, chest sticking out, her rib cage forming a smoothly furred arch that moved slightly with each breath. Her tongue lolled out of her mouth and her eyelids gently twitched. She must be dreaming, Danny thought.

A wintry wind whistled at the windows in the late afternoon, like a ghost faintly pleading to come in from the cold. The ghost of winter. The earth outside was still icy in patches and rock hard, and the squirrels that used to run through the maple and oak trees in the backyard last fall had moved to their nests long ago to sleep away the winter. Soon they would be stirring again. Danny turned back to his diary.

I got my blue belt in judo. Sensei Bob says I need to work harder, and that's okay. He's right. He says it won't be long before I can go for my brown belt, and then on to my black belt. But I'm not sure how long I want to continue doing judo.

Susan went back to university. She got the volleyball scholarship she wanted and she's been a lot more pleasant to me lately. Which I appreciate! Mom is still working as a social worker. She just takes life one day at a time, she says. "People talk about multitasking, but you can only do one thing at a time," she always says to me. And everything is still nice to her.

Every couple of weeks, I go over to Evelyn Jossa Park with Long Shot and look at the place where we scattered Dad's ashes. There's a birch tree that stands alone and I think of it as Dad's tree. I close my eyes and imagine Dad leaning against it, watching the Canada geese on the pond nearby.

I started working part-time at the library, shelving books. It's booooring! But at least I can make some money at it. University will come too soon. I have to get my head around it.

Mr. Mahoney sent me a postcard the other day. "Greetings from Tampa, Florida!" it said. Palm trees and the Gulf of Mexico and deep red sunset across the horizon. Everything is great with him and his dogs are running well. What a nice guy — he said if I ever want to come for a visit I would be welcome — Long Shot too, of course. Maybe we'll go next winter?

As if sensing Danny's thoughts, the greyhound stretched and *thump-thumped* her tail, raised her head slightly, then went back to sleep. Danny's thoughts about the rangy greyhound, relaxing in a way that only dogs can, moved to his stomach. He was getting hungry. Spoon pudding. Maybe there was some in the fridge?

He wandered into the kitchen, found a spoon pudding in the refrigerator, put on his jacket, and wandered outside, into the backyard, his sneakers slipping a bit on the frost-coated grass. Small piles of still-melting snow were heaped here and there. It was that time of year when you could feel the warmth of spring gently sneaking into everything. Danny looked at the afternoon sky. It was lengthening into evening, streaks of indigo and red and purple stretched like strands of ribbon from one end to the other. He thought of Nicole, the purple streaks in her jet-black hair, her smile, the way she teased him, gently, about everyday things. She might be working now. He took his cellphone out of his jacket pocket and texted her. "I ♥ you," he typed.

Eating the spoon pudding, he surveyed the yard. *It's not so bad*, he thought. The sunlight to the west was caught by the branches of a tree, which cast shadows across the patchy ice and snow. Danny squinted his eyes, letting the pastel shades and shadows blend and merge with his mind. He created a tapestry, imagining a great picture of his life stretched across the backdrop of the sky, images in motion from one side to the other: his mother working at the kitchen table, his sister playing volleyball, him earning a belt in judo, a pack of long-limbed dogs racing down a red-dirt track after a mechanical rabbit, and one tall, lean man, studious-looking, with a ponytail and scraggly goatee, standing alone, gently smiling at the scene.

Danny's cellphone vibrated. It was Nicole. "I ♥ you too."

AUTHOR'S NOTE

THE LETTER

All of this work is fiction, with the exception of the letter from Danny's grandfather. Much of the text of that letter is drawn from one written by my great-grandfather Martin to my great-grandmother Alice during the First World War. Martin was a private in the Canadian Corps in Ypres, Belgium, and fought at the Battle of Mount Sorrel in 1916. To me, the letter truly represents courage and dedication, laced with doubt, anxiety, and isolation—capturing the thoughts and feelings of average people who rose to a challenge to do extraordinary things.

GREYHOUNDS

There are many greyhound adoption organizations across Canada and the United States, and they do great work.

For the right family, a retired racing dog makes a wonderful, loving pet. I encourage anyone who is interested in adopting a retired greyhound to find out more by getting in touch with their local organization.

DARFUR

Ben's story of genocide and slavery is sadly typical of the experiences of many young people in the Darfur region of western Sudan. Despite shaky peace agreements, this part of Africa continues to suffer from political instability, war, starvation, and the breakdown of traditional ways of life — all of which create human suffering on a massive scale. Organizations like Canadians Against Slavery and Torture in Sudan (CASTS) have done much to bring this situation to the world's attention and there are many excellent books written on this topic. I urge readers to learn more about Darfur and add their voices to the chorus of those calling for long-term solutions in this part of the world.

More Great Fiction for Young People

FEVER SEASON
by Eric Zweig
978-1554884322
$12.99

It is early 1919 in Montreal and a deadly outbreak of Spanish Influenza has killed thousands. Davis Saifert, a thirteen-year-old English Canadian, is alone: his father died fighting in the First World War and his mother and sister were recent victims of the flu epidemic. But he does have a childhood photo of his mother's long-lost brother, who he thinks lives in Seattle. Luck strikes when David gets a job with the Montreal Canadiens, who earn the right to play the Seattle Metropolitans in the Stanley Cup playoff, allowing David to travel across the country with the hockey club. What fate awaits the mighty Canadiens on the West Coast? Will David find his uncle? Will he survive the deadly flu?

Arctic Thunder
by Robert Feagan
978-1554887002
$12.99

Mike Watson's team has just won the Alberta Bantam Provincial box lacrosse championships. The euphoria of victory and plans for next season are short-lived when Mike's father, a member of the Royal Canadian Mounted Police, is transferred to Inuvik, Northwest Territories. The transition to life inside the Arctic Circle is a tough one. With temperatures of -30 Celsius, a hulking monster named Joseph Kiktorak threatening him at every turn, and not a lacrosse ball in site, Mike's resentment at moving north escalates. But as his friendships with local youth develop, Mike is introduced to the amazing spectacle and athleticism of traditional "Arctic Sports." The idea of an Inuvik lacrosse team is born! With hearts full of desire, the motley group of athletes heads south to participate in the Baggataway Lacrosse Tournament, and to face Mike's former team, The Rams.

DUNDURN
www.dundurn.com

What did you think of this book?
Visit www.dundurn.com
for reviews, videos, updates, and more!